ALLEGIANCE TO THE NEW ORDER

Doyle opened his eyes and gazed upward. The cycling spheroid of pulsing light in the dome overhead descended. He did not dare relax his vigil. He forced his thoughts to remain on the mind code and everything that pertained to it, never for an instant permitting his mind to wander.

An audible voice whirred like the wings of a thousand birds in flight. "Once you have been programmed, you will be under pain of death, committed to forever guard these secrets until the end of your days. Is that understood, Captain Doyle?" At Doyle's nod it continued.

"As of right now you are *un*free. You will no longer function as a free spirit in this or any other community on this planet. Do you wish, for any reason, to withdraw yourself from this nomination? Speak now or forever be silent."

Doyle knew what was expected of him. He had no choice. He pledged that he would nevermore speak out against the regime. But he did not say a word about *acting* against it!

Android Armageddon

by Robert Tralins

PINNACLE BOOKS • **NEW YORK CITY**

Copyright © 1974 by Robert Tralins

An original Pinnacle Books edition, published for the first time anywhere.

ISBN: 0-523-00513-X

First printing, December 1974

Printed in the United States of America

PINNACLE BOOKS, INC.
275 Madison Avenue
New York, N.Y. 10016

Android
Armageddon

1

Android Armageddon

Doyle turned away from the viewing scope, his expression grim, his jaw set with determination. He had decided they still had a chance to escape the net the alien invaders had thrown up around them and that there was still time to warn the earth colony eighteen hundred miles west of them of the imminent danger all life on Pulsar 143 faced.

Doyle's five crewmen aboard the surface exploration craft 214, code name *Tangier*, had been at their posts ever since they had finished hiding the craft in the shifting brown sands of the vast arid plain some thirty hours earlier. Alien spaceships had been landing on the surface around their hiding place, and the crewmen had been observing them in an effort to learn as much as possible about them—where they came from, who they were, and why they had come in force to destroy the small earth colony on Pulsar 143.

When Doyle's men had found the hundred-foot obelisk in the center of that arid, desolate plain so far from the earth colony, they discovered that they had walked into a trap. The moment they had entered the vicinity of the obelisk, a powerful force field had been activated, entrapping them. They could neither send messages out of, nor receive transmissions through, the field. To make matters worse, when they

1

tried to start their engines in the hopes of crashing through the invisible barrier, they discovered that their power had been neutralized. Except for the tiny voltages from the battery banks in the storage compartments that operated their sensors and viewers, nothing was operational.

Later, while observing the landings of wave after wave of spheroid craft, they had intercepted a strange communiqué being broadcast from the spheroid flagship that had landed on the top of the obelisk. They transferred the power from their optical viewers to the auxiliary inputs of the computer and then fed the communiqué into it. A few minutes later it had been translated. *Seek and destroy all alien life!*

There was no doubt in Doyle's mind that the spaceships were capable of destroying all life on the planet. Before landing, the vehicles had swooped down low to emit bursts of blinding light aimed at the earth around the obelisk. These continuous bursts of ray-fire blasted a deep pit in the ground, five hundred yards in diameter. It was obvious to the men that the invaders were testing their firepower while at the same time saluting the flagship.

"Okay," said Webb, Doyle's second in command, "it figures that they're trying out their ray guns and they're saluting the flagship atop that obelisk—but why the pit?"

Matthews, at his optical viewer, looked up and shrugged. He turned and said, "I think we ought to worry about how to get out of here instead of why they're blasting that hole."

Sergeant Jackson, who was standing at the range finder beside Captain Doyle, turned and said, "Matthews makes sense. If we spend our time guessing about that damned hole, we're not going to figure a way out of here. Anybody got any new ideas?"

Captain Doyle grinned and told them, "I think I have."

The five men looked up from their consoles and peered at Doyle. The strain of what they were under showed in their tense expressions.

Doyle swiveled around in his chair and removed the small receiver from his right ear. He held it up and said, "Gentlemen, from the tone of that gibberish we've been intercepting, my guess is that they're blasting that pit to make a construction foundation for some kind of gear they're waiting for." He rose and went to the optical viewer, which was focused on the great pit. He pointed at the excavation and said, "Notice how it seems to be geometrically perfect, almost as though they're making room for a spheroid craft ten times the size of their ships."

Matthews looked into the binocular viewer, adjusted the knobs, and then turned to face them. "Captain Doyle may be right. Except for the flagship on top of the obelisk, which is a hundred yards in diameter, each of the other ships in the fleet measures exactly fifty yards in diameter. For the lack of any other theory, I'm inclined to agree with the captain. They're preparing for the arrival of their command ship."

"What's your opinion?" Sergeant Jackson asked, turning to Lieutenant Webb.

Lieutenant Webb shrugged. He had been calculating the firepower of the arriving UFOs. "I have no opinion," he said flatly. "All I know is that each craft emitted two bursts of ray-fire lasting exactly .08 second. We counted fifty-six ships in the armada. We know they managed to blast out a symmetrically balanced pit exactly five hundred yards in diameter with 112 shots. This kind of pinpoint accuracy and precision convinces me of one thing: we don't stand a chance against them. We've nothing to combat that kind of deadly firepower and no weapon to equal such a thing."

Warrant Officer Matthews frowned. After a moment of deep thought, he said, "Then *why* such elaborate preparation for the arrival of a command ship? Why dig a pit that would bury it up to its equator in the earth?"

Captain Doyle pointed at the viewer and said, "We can only surmise that the aliens are bringing a vessel here to help them

3

annihilate us. Obviously, they consumed a great quantity of power to come here with such speed from wherever they're from. My calculated guess is that this vessel they're expecting is some kind of a refueling or repowering plant. Notice the way the spheroids have spiraled around the pit on the ground." He turned the viewer quickly, and the men could see how the spheroids were indeed lined up in a spiral formation. "Suppose this power plant or whatever it is they're waiting for must be anchored or half-buried—grounded—if it is to refuel the armada?"

Lieutenant Webb jumped up excitedly, interrupting, "That's it, Captain! It's logical that they're in that formation to link up with the command or refueling ship when it lands there."

The two corporals, Slack and Abel, looked at the officers and laughed aloud.

Captain Doyle swiveled around to face them. "What's funny?"

Corporal Slack replied, "Sir, it's too simple to be believable. We don't know anything about those aliens or why they put that obelisk signal beacon out there or why they're here to massacre us—"

"That's just the point," Doyle said sharply. "We don't know what their source of power is, but one thing we do know is that it isn't nuclear. Therefore, it's only logical to assume they must refuel; hence, they've formed up on the ground and made preparations to link up with a command ship or a refueling ship. As to why they put the obelisk on this planet, my guess is they wanted it here for the sole purpose of warning them if other beings came here. I assume they are under orders to seek and destroy us because they believe our presence here is a threat to them—to their existence."

"Then what's so important about this theory?" asked Corporal Slack. "Frankly, I fail to see . . ."

Captain Doyle rose and stood in the center of the bridge.

4

"Gentlemen," he said, "do you agree that the aliens know we're here—hiding from them?"

All heads nodded affirmatively.

"Do you agree that they've not yet begun to search us out and destroy us because it's possible they've exhausted their power and must energize again before they can go after us?"

There was a long silence before everyone nodded in agreement. The thought had not occurred to them before. They were smiling a moment later when they looked at their captain's face.

Doyle went to the viewer and pointed at the spiral formation of the grounded spheroids. "Gentlemen, I think we have a chance not only to get away, but to destroy their fleet as well."

"But that's ridiculous!" cried Lieutenant Webb, leaping to his feet. "We have no weapons—we're an exploration team—we're scientists, not military men."

"It doesn't matter what we are," Doyle said. "We're scientists and that's all that counts. We don't need weapons. They have all we need."

"Explain yourself, Captain." Warrant Officer Matthews sounded annoyed.

Doyle pointed at the location of the spheroid pit, then with a pair of calipers, he measured the distance on the scaled scope. "If we can topple the obelisk onto the command ship when it grounds there—at a strategic moment—we can blow them all up in a spiral chain!"

"But suppose we can't topple the obelisk?" said Matthews.

Captain Doyle pointed to Sergeant Jackson. "Can we do it, Sergeant? Do you think a charge will turn it over?"

The sergeant smiled. He produced several facsimiles of underground photographs he had taken of the obelisk while they were investigating it. He then peeled back the overlays and nodded, holding up one of the thin sheets. "It's buried some ten feet deep at the base. If I can get between it and the crater and plant a big enough charge deep enough, the blast will flip over dead center on the crater."

Doyle looked around at the men. "Gentlemen," he said, "if we're to take action, we have to get busy right now. Are you with me?"

As Doyle turned to face the men, each one nodded in turn. He then assigned them specific tasks and broke open the arms locker and equipment compartments. They strapped on sidearms and exploration gear, survival packs, and communicators. Then Doyle led the way out through the hatch. They had to tunnel out through the brown dust that they had placed over the craft to camouflage it. When they emerged in the daylight, Doyle dispersed the men and then led them across the plain in the direction of the obelisk, taking cover every few feet behind rocks and mounds of dust. He stayed away from the spheroids encircling the obelisk and went down almost to the mouth of the crater in order to avoid detection. Finally, he reached the obelisk. He looked up at the spheroid atop the monumental structure, then suddenly looked away and motioned for the men to hurry across the plain to his side. One by one they quickly ran out and joined him.

As Doyle regained his breath after the exertion, he realized he did not dare think of what might happen to them if they were discovered by the aliens or if their plan failed. He knew he could ill afford to have anything go wrong. He had learned as a boy that difficult tasks are possible only when a man *believes* he can accomplish them. Negative thoughts diminish the chances of success. He broke out his digging gear and began to shovel away the soft, dry dirt at the base of the obelisk. As he worked, Sergeant Jackson prepared the explosive charges, which he placed in cylinders to be lowered into the hole being dug beside the obelisk.

Corporal Abel, standing watch beneath a shelf of rock several yards away, called to them: "They've spotted us. Look up there—a cable elevator!"

6

Doyle dropped the shovel and rushed out beside Abel. He looked up and saw a cable elevator being lowered rapidly from the belly of the spheroid perched a hundred feet above them. He drew his weapon and stood waiting, watching as two androids in gray uniform coveralls descended.

The others at the base of the obelisk had scattered for cover, taking their weapons and tools with them.

The elevator reached the ground and the androids stepped off the platform. They walked down to the base of the crater and peered into it through a transit-type instrument.

"What're they doing?" the corporal asked Doyle in an apprehensive whisper.

"Looks like they're making a final check of the pit. Keep your head, Abel. They might not notice our diggings."

"But all that noise we were making," he said, "and look there—they've got to be blind not to see what we were doing."

"You better hope they're blind to that," Doyle said. He grinned. "Just stand easy. No point worrying about things that might never happen."

"Yes, no point to that," the corporal said.

They watched the androids for several minutes while they slowly rotated the transit around the perimeter of the crater, which had been blasted out of the rock and earth. When they finished surveying it, they folded the tripod legs of the instrument and carried it back to the platform. They stepped onto the platform and were immediately lifted back up to the belly of the spheroid.

When the androids were gone, Doyle and the others assembled at the base of the obelisk. They fell to work again, digging the hole. Corporal Slack and Lieutenant Webb had climbed down into the soft earthen hole beside the obelisk and were working feverishly to reach the bottom. After several minutes the lieutenant tossed his folding shovel out of the hole and asked for the blasting cylinders. The sergeant gingerly lowered them down and watched as the lieutenant placed

7

them along the base of the obelisk. When the cylinders were ready, the two men climbed out of the hole. Everyone busily cooperated, refilling the hole with the silt and heavy brown sand. When the hole had been refilled, they drew back to a place of safety on the plain that overlooked the obelisk and the crater before it. Taking cover behind some boulders, they settled back to await further developments. All around them they could see the gleaming domes of the spheroids, spiraling in an ever-widening formation out from the perimeter of the crater.

Lieutenant Webb was the first to spot the command ship when it appeared on the northern horizon. He pointed, and all eyes turned to stare. It was just as they had surmised—a duplicate of the smaller spheroids but ten times as large. It seemed to be decelerating as it swooped toward them, and when it was directly above the crater, it stopped. There was a moment of dead silence, followed by a loud humming noise, after which the craft began to descend. It finally settled in the crater, and then the humming sound decreased until it was only a few decibels above the sound of the wind sweeping across the plain.

Doyle, with glasses to his eyes, watched the huge ship. A few minutes after it had settled, the top half began to revolve slowly and a stubby, mastlike appendage began to rise out of the center. At the top of the appendage was a glistening, silvery bulb that appeared to be faceted with mirrorlike prisms. A ray of brilliant light shot forth from the appendage and connected with the first ship to the right of the crater. Then Doyle noticed that all the ships in the armada had elevated similar masts. In a blinding flash of light the ray from the great ship connected to each of the craft in a widening spiral.

"That's it," whispered Doyle, signaling the sergeant.

Sergeant Jackson activated the charges, and the men shielded their eyes, awaiting the blast.

Suddenly a low rumbling was heard, and a huge geyser of brown dust shot up around the base of the obelisk. All eyes turned upwards, watching as the obelisk began to topple over, carrying the flagship with it. A moment later the spheroid smashed against the mast that was emitting the beam of light to the alien armada. There was a fearful crackling sound, and suddenly all the craft began to blaze with ray-fire as the recharging device short-circuited like a spiraling pinwheel disintegrating itself.

The men were knocked off their feet by the impact of the shock waves striking them. Doyle and the lieutenant were buffeted into a niche behind the rock. The others were lifted into the air, screaming in pain and surprise. A moment later the entire plain had exploded in a blaze of dazzling white light. Then a gigantic whirlwind, a dust storm shaped like an inverted tornado was set into motion.

Doyle and Webb were buried under shale and brown dust. The others in the crew vanished, as did the spheroids, the obelisk, and the crater.

Silence followed. The wind slowly died, and the dust rained down silently like brown silicon snow.

Beneath the rubble and the dust, Doyle and Webb lay unconscious in a crevice.

Time passed.

Doyle regained consciousness and crawled over to Webb. He shook him and slapped his face, reviving him. Webb awakened, rubbing dust from his eyes, blinking, sneezing, and choking. He finally pulled himself together, and they began the tedious job of digging themselves out. They were exhausted when they reached the surface, but their physical exhaustion was forgotten when they found themselves gazing out on total emptiness. Everything had been obliterated. The obelisk and the flagship atop it had disintegrated a moment after it struck the refueling craft, which in turn destroyed the entire alien fleet.

9

They saw no one alive; no trace of life or man-made craft or alien invader.

When they had regained their composure, Doyle led the way down to the plain where they had buried their surface craft. They searched for it with sensors from their survival packs. Finally they located it. Before the blast, the craft had been buried under only a few inches of dust. But now it was down twenty-five feet. Doyle and Webb fell to work in silence, digging slowly and steadily. Several times the walls of the powdery brown sand and dust collapsed around them in the pit they were digging and they had to begin anew. Neither man bothered to complain. To do so would have been a waste of precious energy. They knew that if they were to survive the swiftly approaching night and the one hundred degrees below zero cold that always came with it, they would have to reach shelter.

Finally, with just a few minutes of daylight left, Doyle's spade touched the *Tangier*'s entry hatch. They fell to work with renewed vigor, and when the dirt and brown powder had been cleared away, they opened the door and went into the dark interior, clamping the airtight door shut behind them.

The systems were fully operational, unharmed by the holocaust that had destroyed the alien fleet. Doyle turned on the power, and at once the craft became habitable. Webb, too weary to refresh himself with a food packet from the console dispenser, dropped into the copilot's seat, flipped the lever that folded it out into a couch, and fell asleep at once.

Doyle forced himself to make a final check of the systems before he opened out his chair-couch and dropped wearily across it. As he sank into sleep, he was conscious of the purring of the idling rotor recharging the power banks and he thought about searching for his crew—or what remained of it—first thing the next morning.

2

Transient Citadel

Captain Doyle stood on the balcony outside his chambers on the thirty-third level. He leaned against the railing and gazed down on the City of Mnemosyne, which stretched before him in reality just as the confrontation with the alien invaders was now, in memory, behind him.

In contemplation his youthful face appeared grim and angry. He was not at all pleased, because he had been ordered back to the colony, and he was disgusted and angered because he had been informed, immediately on his arrival from the barren plains of the frontier, that he was relieved of his command and was permanently returned to citizen status.

In the first gray light of morning that swept the planet from directly overhead, dissolving the red mists of night, new dimensions of age and wisdom seemed to be added to his features. Despite the seventeen years he had spent on Pulsar 43 since that eerie dawn in 2083 when the transport had landed the first colonists on the planet, he had never quite gotten over the sensation of discomfort and uneasiness whenever night faded into the breaking dawn. Now more than ever he was aware of the uncanniness of it. One minute it was night—the next, precisely at 0600 each morning, the daystar moved from behind the six regents of night and blotted them from view one by one at sixty-second intervals until at exactly 0606 the glassy skies were devoid of glowing roons, and it was day.

The roons were natural satellites and not true moons since they exerted no magnetic attraction on the planet and were little more than gigantic flattened discs of cooling volcanic rock in perfect circular orbit, revolving once every twelve hours around Pulsar 143. The phenomenon occurred with such precision, that all chronographs were set · by it, and it had become the standard mean time for all colonists.

And then the nimbus of day broke like a colossal pinwheel unraveling brightening streamers of vapor that thinned as it spun off in vanishing ribbons over the flat horizon. Next came the brilliant sunlit warmth not unlike that of the earth's sun, which rose so majestically each day in the eastern horizon of his native world, he recalled nostalgically. He missed watching the sunrise as he had often observed it during the months prior to his final departure from earth. It was not that he was homesick and yearned to see once again the relatives he remembered and the friends of his youth; instead, he was weary of the way things had turned out. Instead of being honored for what he had done, it seemed that he was being punished for it. He dreaded the thought of giving up his command—and worse than that, he was dismayed at the thought of living the rest of his life in subservience and obedience, of following the orders of others. Such was the fate that a demoted captain might expect.

Somehow he had never been able to accept the new order of things, which his fellows had so readily accepted, approved, and adapted themselves to follow. Something in the recesses of his memory that he could not define prevented him from enjoying the same contented outlook and peace of mind that his comrades everywhere seemed to experience. He could not understand what was so different about himself. He could not

12

d it within himself to sit idly by while the newcomers
dermined all that had been decided and established when
e planet had first been colonized. He was unable to sit and
atch all that he and his fellow settlers had sacrificed so much
built being taken over by the newcomers. He had to do
mething. He could not stand still for this.

He had been recalled from the outer reaches of the planet
was exploring to the transient citadel and confined to his
arters allegedly because the Secretariat now wished to
view what had taken place on the plain during the
nfrontation with the alien invasion fleet. He was vexed by
is and knew something strange was afoot because Lieutenant
ebb had been spirited away to the Secretariat's chambers and
d not been heard from since.

Doyle was also disturbed by what he now saw stretched out
fore him to the four quadrants of the horizon. The city that
and the other settlers had built and then settled before he
d moved off to the outer reaches of the planet had
dergone vast and drastic changes. From the transient citadel
the city central where he was now overlooking the Gardens
Mnemosyne to the bleak moors at the edge of the suburbs,
erything had been changed. He could hardly believe his eyes.
lthough he had heard frequent reports during the long years
had spent on the frontiers that the Secretariat had been
stematically reorganizing all things, he had not imagined
ey had accomplished this much or gone so far. From what
could see, there was reason enough for being displeased at
eing back.

The opening of the arch behind him heralded the arrival of
e servomaid that had been assigned him. The practice of
ssigning a servomaid or servoman to guests of the citadel had
een inaugurated during the early days of the colony
ttlement.

The automated girl, laden down with the tray she had been

programmed to prepare in the community galley on the thirty-third level and then serve to him, stood immobile awaiting his instructions.

Doyle moved to the small table at the far corner of the balcony and seated himself on a bench before it. He gestured for the girl to place the tray on the table and watched as she came forward, her supple figure and slender limbs moving gracefully beneath the sheer cloth of the duty dress uniform she was wearing.

"What are you called?" he asked as she placed the dishes of food before him in the correct arrangement.

"I am called Charity, sir," she said with lowered eyes. "Number six-four-one, Servomaid thirty-third level, suite B."

"How long have you been here?" He asked in an offhanded manner as he dipped a spoon into the sealed top of the vitamized yoghurt container and stirred the contents.

"I am number six-four-one and that is my age, sir."

Doyle glanced at her as he tasted the first spoonful. He remembered that the servopeople had been indoctrinated to live by time beginning with the date or number of their rebirth. When he had learned of the process and the plan to supply the population with servoworkers whose minds were several degrees below the intelligence of androids, he had rebelled against the idea. He found the plan to automate quasihumans reprehensible, and for this reason he had decided to join the exploration forces. He did not wish to belong to the society of men who were repeating the errors of former societies; societies from which those who formed the first colony movement were seeking to escape. But how did Doyle know that? He wondered about this, thinking of himself in the third person. He asked it of himself several times. Somewhere, somehow, deep within the recesses of his memory, Doyle *knew*. And somehow he knew he was not supposed to know.

He recalled that the immigration of servoservants had spread to all divisions of the colony, and during the past decade, to

e outposts on the frontiers as well. Although he had learned
 accept them, he could not bring himself to treat his servant
 a material thing—a piece of equipment or machinery—as did
s colleagues. To Doyle, they were beings, living bipeds,
eatures, androids, or lower man. He could not think of them
herwise. He did not want to think of them the same way his
llows did. He wanted to forget some of the teachings he had
quired in his youth—but the word *forget* in all its tenses was
boo on Pulsar 143. It was considered a cardinal sin for any
ember of the society to utter the words, "I forgot." This was
nderstandable because the society had been founded on the
oncept that man's mind when it remembered and used all the
nowledge programmed into it was supreme—and perhaps if
eveloped along this concept, all future generations would be
nuinely so—hence, the Mind Code had become the regimen
r all citizens to live by and even die for.

Within the tenets of the mind code, to possess a photo-
raphic memory was considered the highest achievement
tainable and the ideal all were dedicated to strive toward.
hose with prodigious mental powers were honored as the
oblest citizens of all, and they received—commensurate with
eir abilities to recall—position, fame, and power as their civic
wards.

"Will there be anything else, sir?" the servomaid asked.

"For the present, that will be all," Doyle said. "I'll buzz if I
ant you."

"Six-four-one on the viewer panel is my call number, sir."
he began to back toward the door, bowing in deference.
oyle cursed under his breath when he saw her do this. It
nnoyed him because such subservient gestures and behavior
elonged in some decadent empirical society back on earth—
ot here on Pulsar 143. He had no idea how he knew this
ither, but somehow he knew it, and the knowledge bedeviled
im like a miniscule leak of current in an electronic module
hat one knows is present, but cannot locate.

15

"All right, Charity," he said.

There was no emotion, no expression of surprise in the servomaid's face as she continued to back out of the room. "I return now to the section where I am quartered, sir."

Doyle watched her until she turned and vanished beyond the arch. Despite his many years on the planet, he still could not adjust to the thought that thousands of workers and servants just like Charity, number six-four-one, who had been brought to the colonies during the past decade, were devoid of creative thought—mindless humanoids, automated creatures re-created solely to fill a labor need on the planet. He found it difficult to conceive of how it was for them to be as they were—without minds of their own. He remembered something of early earth history, of how the European crossed the Atlantic and colonized the North and South American continents, building his civilizations there with bondservants and Negro slaves. Now the space colonists had gone their forebears one better: they were not exploiting other men—instead they were using humanoid machines manufactured with computer minds instead of human minds. The great new world they had begun on Pulsar 143 was not about to become a hotbed for revolution as had the nations on earth. They had created servopeople who were mentally and intellectually incapable of disobedience or insurrection.

The metallic signal of the communicator ring on his left hand abruptly brought his thoughts back to the present. He touched the tiny emblem, activating the microceiver. "Yes?"

"Is that you, Doyle?" a feminine voice inquired. It was a voice from the past. A voice that brought a surge of color to Doyle's cheeks, and his pulse quickened. "Is it *really* you, darling?"

"Petra!" he smiled at the microreceiver. "Where are you?"

"Here in Mnemosyne, where else?"

"That's great. But how come? I thought you were permanently stationed out there—never to return."

16

"Things have changed. But that's not important. What about you, Doyle? How are you? Now that you're a hero, you just have plenty to—"

"Hero?" he laughed sourly. "Where'd you get that idea?"

"I heard all about it—how you almost single-handedly got rid of the android invaders and how you and Webb were the only survivors. It was on all the viewers—the obelisk out there and the spheroid ships—everything. We saw it all—even the Armageddon."

For a moment Doyle was speechless. He hadn't known that the encounter had been monitored. Then he remembered how Webb and Jackson had staked out the plain with viewing cameras. He had forgotten all about that. He was puzzled now, and he couldn't think of anything to say.

"Doyle, you haven't answered me. How are you?"

"Fine," he said. "I was never better."

"You don't sound too happy, though. Is something the matter?"

"Well, since you ask, something *is* the matter. I've been relieved of my command. Cashiered from the service."

She laughed. "Oh, is that all?"

He frowned. "Isn't that enough?"

"You poor darling," she said, still laughing. "You don't know?"

"Know *what?*" he said, growing impatient. The lines at the edge of his jaw tightened and his eyes narrowed. "What's going on, Petra? What's this all about? The way they've been treating me is puzzling—to say the least."

She laughed. "Don't let it bother you, darling. I'll explain as soon as I come over. Right now I'm at father's. I was about to drop in and surprise you, but decided I'd better not. I understand those voluptuous servomaids are something else."

"That," he said with amused annoyance, "isn't fair. You ought to know me better than that. If a woman isn't the real thing, I don't waste my time."

17

Her voice sounded like a little girl's in the microceiver. "Silly one, when're you going to learn to stop taking everything so seriously? I was only joking."

Doyle stretched and rose from the table. He reentered the chambers, a smile on his lips. He was so anxious to see Petra again after such a long time that he could barely wait for her to get there. He chose freshly laundered slacks and a jerkin from the folding bag he had brought. As he completed his toilet, shaved, and took a sonic-shower, he wondered if he and Petra would be able to spend some time together, perhaps even go away on a holiday for a few days. It had been a long, long time since he had been free of responsibilities, and he welcomed the chance to relax for a while—to live as a man instead of a commander. Ever since he had been put in command of Exploration Outpost 1264, code name *Tangier*, his whole life had been wrapped up in the duties of his task, and he had resigned himself to the fact that little hope remained for him and Petra to be together again as they had been in the old days.

He wondered if Petra had in some manner induced her father, the citadel commandant, to exert his influence over the Secretariat to have him returned here, but he doubted if she had had anything to do with it. Knowing Petra's father, old fiery-eyed Bodmew, Doyle was confident even Petra, his daughter, would be unable to influence him. Deciding it would accomplish little to think about it, he discarded his robe—and his thoughts—and dressed in a fresh suit of thermal underwear, and then donned the outfit he had unpacked.

As Petra emerged from the vestibule of the transportation tube some minutes later, all thought of the events that had transpired during the past few days vanished from his mind. He caught her up in his arms, and they kissed, embracing each other as though nothing else mattered and nothing had happened during the long months of their separation.

As they stood on the balcony later, gazing down at the

processions of people streaming on the moving sidewalks far below, going to and from the Gardens of Mnemosyne, traveling from their quarters to their places of employment, attending classes in the lecture domes, or partaking of the amusements in the amphitheaters, the bistros, and game parks, Petra sighed and rested her head on Doyle's shoulder. "You know, darling," she said with moody concern, "if you'd only conform and stop being so reactionary—then perhaps the Secretariat might see fit to transfer you back here permanently."

Doyle moved away from her and grasped her oval face between his hands. He tilted her face so he could gaze into her eyes. "Be honest, Petra," he said, "did the Secretariat have anything to do with sending you here—to be with me?"

She averted her gaze. A moment later she reached up and gently pushed his hands from her face, but clung to them, her fingernails digging into his flesh. She sighed. "I shan't try to deceive you, dearest one. Yes, the Secretariat *is* responsible for our reunion. They granted me time off to enjoy this holiday with you—provided I agreed to try to influence your thinking. I knew you would be on to me, but I came anyway. At the risk of alienating you, I agreed. I never could fool you. Do you blame me? Are you angry?"

"No," Doyle smiled. "You tried before, remember?"

"Let's not talk about that. Times have changed since then. Ever since the Justivac was programmed to replace the government, everything has changed. Don't you see—it's no longer wise or expedient to be a dissident. The buffoonery of being led by elected officials is ended. Now we are led by the machine, and it's better this way. Justice for all is now a reality. So why not accept the new order of things like all the others? Why continue being stubborn and contrary? Haven't you learned by now you can't fight it?"

"No," Doyle said, folding his arms and contemplating her pretty face. "I'll never accept being enslaved by a computer. I don't care if all the wisdom of a hundred civilizations has been programmed into it. It's the principle of the thing. Blind obedience to the Justivac is just another form of slavery."

"Slavery?" she cried. "We've never been freer."

"You can't mean that," he said, peering into her eyes as though trying to read her innermost thoughts. "Surely you can't agree that we're free when we're ruled by an electronic brain that does all our thinking for us—that rules our very lives!"

"It's infallible," her eyes searched his for some sign that she was getting to him. "It's infallible, darling. Man isn't perfect—but the machine is. This simple philosophy is enough to convince me—and most everyone here on Pulsar 143—that man shouldn't govern his fellow man if he's less than perfect. We all deserve a fair chance, and the Justivac ensures that we get this chance—provided everyone conforms to its regulations."

Doyle nodded, openly refusing to accept her statement. "How can you let yourself be duped this way?"

"Darling, what's gotten into you?"

He nodded again. "I can't conform, Petra. Something in me refuses to let me accept this rule by a machine." He gazed absently at the gardens far below. "I remember the old days and what we were building then. I've seen all the old guard become lackeys to the new order. We've been betrayed." He turned and fixed his gaze on her. "I'm different from the others, and different from you because I still remember my native world and how it was to live under governments of men—not machines. The memory traces of my heritage are still in my mind. I'm not so fortunate as you and the others who have been born here. I feel that I must speak out against the Secretariat because it betrayed us the day it turned over the reins of government to the Justivac. I must protest, I must warn everyone of the consequences if we go on this way, obeying the edicts of a damned machine. Why can't you understand my view, Petra? Why must you and all the others follow so blindly the edict of the Secretariat and that infernal computer? Why can't you understand that we didn't settle this new world just to enslave ourselves again? This was supposed to be a free new world, free of greed and avarice, and free of people whose will to power drives them to dominate others. Now that we've achieved this, why should we be enslaved by a machine?"

"We're not enslaved by the Justivac," she said. "We're *guided* by it. That's the difference. That's where you're wrong."

Doyle laughed. "No matter what terminology, the Justivac is still the master and we're its slaves."

"That's not true! We're *free* human beings. We have the freedom to do anything. We're at liberty to come and go as we please."

"If that's so," Doyle told her flatly, "why have you been trying to make me conform? Why did you just say it isn't wise for me to be a reactionary? Why have you been arguing that I ought to stop fighting the machine? If we have all this freedom you're talking about, how come I haven't the right to protest, to rebel, if I want to?" He waited and saw that she was not about to reply. Then he went on, "Why can't *you* see it from *my* point of view? Can't you see how this new world we've settled is on the path to becoming a worse place to live in than the old one we emigrated from seventeen years ago?"

Petra stood nodding in the negative, not accepting what he was saying, refusing now to listen. The moment he stopped talking she embraced him. "Darling, why can't you see things from *our* point of view? We're the majority. You're in the minority. I doubt if there's anyone on this planet who shares your views, so why fight it? Why must you continue to cling to those old concepts of the individuality of man? Don't you know by now that man cannot rule himself? When we entered the red shift, it was seventeen years ago by your chronology, but by ours it was a century ago. Can't you see *our* viewpoint? We're different from you."

"It doesn't make any difference," he said. "We are earthlings from the same stock. The fact that time is stationary for me and on a different plane from yours is no reason for you and those of your generation and the two generations preceding yours to surrender your individuality and become subservient to that machine. Whether we're one generation or ten removed from the original settlers from earth, we ought to hold onto the freedoms we brought with us—that we established as our most sacred right."

"You're exasperating!"

"Why? Because I don't see it your way? Aw, come on, Petra. I still remember all that you and the rest of you have willingly had erased from your memories—"

She clapped her fingers to his lips, silencing him. "Shh!" she cried in apprehension, glancing about them. "Such talk is treason. If anyone should hear you speaking of memory traces from the old life . . ."

Doyle moved away from her, smiling. "There, you see? You've surrendered what little precious freedom you once had. Now you live in mortal fear."

She was exasperated, and it showed in her expression as she contemplated him, in silence, unable to continue her argument.

"I'm sorry it has to be like this, Petra," Doyle said. "I must speak my mind. I don't believe it's right for anyone to stand idly by and let things like this happen without so much as a cry of protest. We're watching this colony and the others we've founded on the frontiers being led right down the road to totalitarianism. The original concepts on which the colony was established have been undermined because a foolhardy council has entrusted a machine to rule us—to administrate our very lives. I can't in good conscience stand by and let this happen."

"Then I pity you," she said with a touch of vehemence.

"Why?" he asked.

"Because you'll be fighting a battle you can't win. The Secretariat has already been warned about your revolutionary tendencies, darling. They *are* watching you. Even if you are a hero, if you continue this sort of insurgent talk, they'll make you pay for it."

"But suppose I'm not alone? Suppose there are others who'll join me?"

Petra laughed. She tossed her head and stood with hands on her hips. "And suppose there are none? Suppose you're the only one who's foolhardy enough to fight the system?"

"Then I'll go it alone if I have to."

She moved toward him and placed her hands on his shoulders. "Dearest," she said with a deep sigh, "don't be a fool. You've too much intelligence for this sort of thing. The cards have been placed face up on the table. Can't you see that? It isn't half as bad as you make it out to be. Give it a chance and let me show you a few things. After we've vacationed here for a few days, you'll change your mind—I just know you will. When you see that at last we've attained perfection in our government and in our society—"

"*Perfection?*" he cried. "How can you of all people say such a thing? We aren't perfect. Perfection is only an ideal—nothing more. Humans aren't perfect. Therefore it's simple logic to know that you can't get perfection out of *im*perfection. Even the machine is imperfect, if you want to labor the point."

"Labor the point?" she cried, gesturing with indignation. "I'll have you know that the Justivac *is* perfect. From its administration we achieve perfection in all matters. It is infallible. It is programmed not to err, and it directs the Secretariat and all the people without error."

"But how about the justice of it all?"

"Justice?" she exclaimed, her eyes wide as she studied him. "So long as we abide by the law we can expect justice. But when we disobey the law, we can also expect justice."

"Let every crime fit the punishment, every argument be solved by the formula—is that it?"

"You sound bitter," she observed.

He nodded and stared hard at her. "You can't be serious, Petra. Not you. Not the girl I've loved ever since we were at the university together. Not the level-headed, free-thinking girl who always took a stand against anyone and anything standing in the way of our personal freedom . . ."

She nodded and held up a hand to silence him. "Say no more, darling. Come with me and see with your own eyes that times have changed and that, as the cliché goes, it pays to join those you can't beat—especially when you're a minority of one."

"And how do you know I'm a minority of one?"

She smiled patronizingly. "Take my word for it, you are."

"But *how* do you know?"

"No one would dare jeopardize their safety so much as you, my dear. No one has ever dared to speak out against the Secretariat or the new order or the Justivac. The vote was cast and it was unanimous. The Justivac won in a free election and received every vote cast."

"I don't believe it."

"I don't care if you do or not. The fact remains that the Justivac won in a free election."

Doyle eyed her suspiciously. "I heard about that election. Forty percent of the population bothered to vote. Sixty percent were too busy with other matters to cast their ballots. The Justivac won because those who didn't vote were the ones responsible for electing it."

She laughed. "You see? That's just the point. With so many apathetic people in our colonies we had no choice but to elect an infallible leader that would govern us in all matters. That's why the Justivac has become so much a guiding power for us all."

Doyle blinked. For all his effort he had accomplished nothing. He realized it would be futile to continue arguing with her. She was beyond reason. She had become a fanatic follower, and it was too late to convert her. Even when she had been a student at the university, she had been the same obstinate person she was now—especially when she was convinced she was right. He decided to say no more about his ideas and pretend to go along with her. But he had one reservation. He would wait until the time was right—*then* he would act.

And he would know what to do.

3

Orrery

Petra and Doyle emerged from the citadel and walked onto the great plaza toward the huge crowd of people that had gathered. Although he had no idea why so many people were present, he was acutely aware of a change in Petra's manner and of something else. Many of the officials who were usually in their offices at that hour were formed up in ranks outside the plaza.

Suddenly over the loudspeakers came a great clamor and the fanfare of trumpets. At his side, Petra began to laugh excitedly. She clutched his arm and shouted up to him, "Surprise! The celebration is to honor you, Captain Doyle!"

A group of uniformed aides moved toward them, smiling and saluting. A man in the uniform of an adjutant came forward with a portable rostrum and placed it in front of Doyle. He smiled and said, "The people expect to hear a few words from you—the hero who saved our world from the alien invaders."

Petra's arms stiffened as she gave Doyle a gentle push toward the rostrum. Doyle, completely flabbergasted, looked around him. Huge mobs of people were swarming toward him across the plaza from every direction. Lines of honor guards who had just quick-marched onto the plaza formed up ranks and joined hands to hold back the crowds. An ear-shattering shout went up from them.

It was like a human stampede the way the throngs were running toward him. People were shouting his name. Others were waving the small banner of the Exploration Force. Some were waving their arms or their caps. Others were trying to push their way through the cordon of guardsmen.

Doyle stepped up to the rostrum and held up his arms. The shouting and cheering became a tumultuous thunder. He finally began to speak. A silence fell over the crowds like a rippling wave.

"I don't know what to say," Doyle began. He turned and looked around at the people. It was a sea of upturned faces. He felt awkward and uncomfortable, and he began to perspire. "This is certainly a surprise. I hardly deserve such tribute . . ."

The cheering of the crowds began anew.

When he spoke again after several minutes, the cheering abated and he was heard above the furor. "I only did what any man in my position would have done. Much of the credit goes to my crew—to Lieutenant Webb and the others—the good men who gave their lives . . ."

At this the mobs went berserk. The guardsmen had to redouble their efforts to restrain them, to keep them back from the center of the plaza. The pressing crowds to the right of the plaza broke through the ranks of the guards and converged toward them. A second cordon of guardsmen quickstepped to the edge of the plaza a few yards from where Doyle and Petra stood on the lectern. At that moment, just as they formed a human barricade and halted the onrushing crowd, several objects went flying through the air and struck Doyle on the head and shoulders. He drew back, startled. The guardsmen turned and pointed their shock sticks at the crowd. The people fell back, dispersing at once without dallying to argue. They knew only too well the pain of the shock sticks, and the sight of them brought fear into their eyes.

Doyle, wiping away the sloppy, wet garbage that had struck him, caught a glimpse of several angry faces in the dispersing crowd. One of the men shook a fist at him and shouted above the tumult, "Secretariat stooge!"

A second man hurled something at Doyle and yelled, "We don't need any more of your kind!" The man vanished in the swarm of people.

Petra shouted above the uproar, "We'd better get out of here!"

Doyle led her back toward the citadel in the midst of a double rank of guardsmen. They entered the archway and stepped onto a moving sidewalk that sped them around the circular building toward the central city.

The moving sideway finally tracked around to the plaza beneath the great dome of the inner city. They got off amid crowds of citizens and servopeople who were going about their business in grim silence, hurrying to the centers of commerce and education along the mall. No one gave Doyle or Petra so much as a second glance.

Doyle could not reconcile himself to what had happened. If there were some in the city who were opposed to what the Secretariat had imposed on them, then he was certain he had just seen at least two of them. This was in some small way gratifying to him, for it meant that he was not alone in his struggle against the tyrannical actions of the Secretariat. He decided to dismiss it from his mind. Before long he would make his move, but until then, he would be better off if he did not consciously think about it.

As he walked beside Petra on their way through the mall, he stared at the faces of the passersby with no little degree of concern. Despite his resolution to put the matter of the dissidents out of his mind, he could not help wondering how many he might find among the multitudes and then enlist. Now and then he glimpsed a familiar face, but when no glance of recognition was returned, despite the fact that the passerby had looked directly at him, he became conscious of a growing feeling of hopelessness. How could he reach the unreachable? Had the Secretariat succeeded in erasing the memories of all those he might recruit as allies?

He had not realized until that morning that the indoctrination of the new order had been so effective or so widespread. He realized that by some quirk of fortune he had missed being indoctrinated by the mind code. Just how this had happened he had no idea. However, he knew he had to find out if there were others who believed as he did. With allies, there might be a chance of fighting the new order. But the idea was staggering. What could he do against so many thousands? Perhaps it was a hopeless dream. Perhaps Petra was right.

They crossed over a footbridge that led them over a vast amphitheater in which a hundred musicians were playing a spirited symphony that he recognized as the *Ballet Suite* by Delibes. He remembered having heard it many years before at the university. Now they were playing the Mazurka Prelude. He took Petra's hand and they paused.

She smiled up at him. "It's been a long time, hasn't it?"

He made no reply. After they listened for a time, she pulled him away. "We'll come back if you like. I can get reserved seats for the evening performance."

"At least this hasn't changed," he said, falling into step beside her. They walked across to a moving sidewalk and were sped along through the environs of the mall toward the scenic gardens of the inner city. When they reached the entrance and stepped onto the decelerator transport, a slowly moving walk that conveyed them around the pillars and terminated at the garden gate, Petra halted and held Doyle by the sleeve as she waved to a tall man in gray coveralls who was walking rapidly toward them.

"You remember Captain Kagan, don't you, darling?" she asked, drawing Doyle toward her.

"I haven't had the pleasure," Doyle said, watching as the man approached, ignoring him, but his eyes raptly upon Petra.

He caught up both her hands in his own and bent to kiss her cheek.

The brazenness of Kagan's intimate caress infuriated Doyle. He did not know why, but he was seized with an intense feeling of hatred for the man, though he knew he had nothing to be jealous about. There was a quality of hostility in Kagan's manner and in the way he pretended Doyle did not exist, not even dignifying him with so much as a polite nod of greeting; he was certain that Kagan had an ulterior motive. Watching them as they spoke, not hearing what they were saying, Doyle sensed the feeling of affection that passed between Petra and Kagan, and this gave him a sense of loss. Now he was uncertain of Petra's feelings toward him. He thought he knew everything about her, about her friends and co-workers, but Kagan was a surprise. Why hadn't she mentioned him before? Why hadn't Doyle heard of the man before this chance encounter?

He decided not to let it bother him, but he knew it would continue to nettle him. He had a feeling that the meeting was not accidental—that Kagan had intentionally arranged to meet them, for what reason he had no idea.

They walked through the garden entrance and entered the labyrinth, Petra strolling between the two men, an arm linked through Doyle's arm, her right hand holding Kagan's left. She paused several times to gaze up at Kagan, then at Doyle. After a time she said, "Captain Kagan is the first officer at the Orrery, you know."

"No, I didn't know," Doyle said. He turned his attention to the gardens and the statuary, trying to arrest his disturbed emotions.

"Doyle doesn't know it yet," Petra said gaily, addressing Kagan but speaking for Doyle's benefit, "but the Secretariat has been considering Captain Doyle for the post of Orrery commandant.

Doyle halted and disengaged Petra's arm from his own. "What?" he demanded.

Petra smiled and glanced quickly around from Kagan. She

31

spoke softly, her eyelids fluttering, "Darling, it was to be another surprise. The Secretariat has been considering you for the post as recompense for what you did out on the plains. It's about time they repaid you for your years of service on the frontiers—and for your heroism. The life of Orrery commandant here in Mnemosyne could be idyllic."

Doyle looked squarely at Kagan. He wondered why Petra had chosen that moment to break the news. "Why did you go to so much trouble to meet us today? I take it this meeting was prearranged?"

Kagan laughed. He waved a hand and looked down at Petra. "It was her idea."

Doyle frowned. He was perplexed and it showed in his face.

Petra turned and nodded at Kagan, signaling him to leave them for a few moments. Without a word Kagan turned his back and moved out of earshot.

Petra raised her hands to Doyle's shoulders. She probed his expression with a searching gaze. "Please don't misunderstand, dearest," she began, "but I asked Kagan to join us in the hopes that he might help me get through to you. I asked him to be with us when I broke the news about your new appointment. You see, I didn't want you to antagonize the Secretariat by turning down such an offer. I know how obstinate you can be."

"And Kagan? What has he to do with it? Why did you ask him in the first place? Is there something between you two?"

She laughed. "We're nothing except friends. But that's beside the point. I thought that after you got used to the idea, Kagan could brief you on the duties and whatnot."

"I don't appreciate this," he said. His voice was thick with contained anger, and he glanced toward Kagan, who was standing several yards from them, gazing down at a floral arrangement beside the walk. He returned his attention to Petra. "What gave you the idea I was ready to be put out to pasture in a cushy desk job?"

"I thought you'd rather welcome the idea of being around people again. I thought you might even settle down and start making plans about marriage."

"We went all through that before," Doyle said. "I thought the matter was settled. That the two of us . . ."

Petra was crestfallen. She lowered her eyes and after several moments removed her hands from his shoulders. "Forgive me for still trying," she said. "I thought there was still hope for us."

"Please, don't let's go into that again." He paused and looked in Kagan's direction. The man was looking at them, a sour expression on his face. Doyle chuckled. "It appears to me your friend Kagan doesn't approve of me."

Petra's eyes were ablaze when she replied, "You're right. He doesn't approve of you. How would *you* like it if an outsider were brought in to take over the commandant's job when by all rights it should be your job? Just because you're a national hero now, you're about to be honored with that job."

"So why did you bring him along? To rub his nose in it? Is he *that* beholden to you?"

Petra moved back a step. "Doyle!" she hissed, "you're impossible! I've gone to all this trouble to try to help you—for old time's sake—for what used to be between us—and this is how you repay me. I thought we meant something to each other, and I thought there still was some hope for you to change, but now I know I'm wrong. You really are a reactionary—an obstinate rebel—a Don Quixote who continues to battle windmills."

Doyle smiled. "I won't be bought with a cushy desk job. I won't be bribed into silence."

"How noble!"

"Are you angry because I've the courage of my convictions and you haven't? Are you arguing with me to justify what you've done, Petra?"

"What've *I* done?" she cried.

"You've sold your soul to the Secretariat just like in the old song—*I owe my soul to the company store.*"

She glared, hands on her hips. "You lunkhead! You of all people ought to know better. I've carried a torch for you so long that I feel like a statue. Yes, I asked Kagan to meet us here. I wanted him to reason with you—because I still care for you. I don't want you to do something idiotic, like declining the Orrery job. I don't suppose you believe that, you boob! And to labor the point, I'll also admit that Kagan cares for me. But he knows he hasn't a chance as long as you're around."

"In other words you want me to join the establishment—to accept the commandant's post?"

"Yes."

"Why? For God's sake, Petra, *why?*"

"I won't go into that now." She paused and glanced around apprehensively, as though aware of a thousand unseen eyes spying on them. For the first time since they had been together, Doyle became aware of her uneasiness. Finally she said, "Darling, can't you for once trust me and do as I ask?"

"What do you want?"

"Just trust me. Accept the Orrery post and bide your time. I'm sorry, but I can't say more."

"I don't know," he said. "I was brought here almost under house arrest, not because the Secretariat wished to honor me, but because they disapprove of my views. I'm not a fool, Petra. I know that gathering for me outside the citadel was an impromptu thing that backfired, but it was supposed to influence me into joining the Secretariat."

"You were never more wrong."

He eyed her and glanced toward Kagan. Then he said, "All right, if it's that important to you, I'll go along. I'll even accept the Orrery post."

"And you won't talk like a radical?"

"I ought to take offense at that, but I won't. Okay, I'm

34

curious. I won't speak out against the regime—but I also won't speak out for them. Is that clear?"

"Perfectly," she said, smiling in pleasure. "Then it's settled?"

He nodded. She turned and beckoned for Kagan to rejoin them. He nodded slowly and moved toward them. For the first time since they had met, Kagan looked up at Doyle's face. "Welcome aboard," he said.

Doyle grinned, but no amusement was in his eyes. "This is good of you, Kagan, to meet us like this."

"Let's get this straight, Doyle," Kagan said. "I'm not doing this out of the goodness of my heart." He glanced longingly at Petra, then went on. "I'm doing this because I want Petra to be happy. During the years I've known her—and cared about her—all she ever talked about was you. I stuck by her in the belief that one day she might give up, but I realize now that might never happen. She's blessed—or cursed—with a kind of tenacity I've never seen before. I only hope you're half the man she believes you to be. I even hope—"

"Kagan!" Petra cried, "stop this." She moved between Doyle and Kagan and gazed at both of them in turn. "I want you both to be friends—to like each other."

Doyle smiled. He spoke to Kagan, but his eyes were raptly fixed on Petra. "You went to a great deal of trouble to arrange the Orrery appointment for me, didn't you, Kagan? Don't tell me you did it just to please Petra. What was the real reason?"

Kagan started to speak but contained his anger. He kept his hands at his sides, clenching and unclenching his fists. "You deserve to be—"

"Doyle!" Petra cried, grabbing his wrist to restrain him. "Try to understand what we're doing for you."

Doyle frowned. He eyed her, nodding in confusion.

"Do you want me to tell him?" Kagan asked her.

"No, I will. He deserves to know the truth." She looked up

at Doyle and said, "We weren't certain how you'd take it, but the Secretariat *ordered,* yes, I said, *ordered* Kagan and me to see to it that you kept your mouth shut and accepted the commandant's post. They cannot afford to have a hero such as you, the great Captain Doyle, branded a traitor in the eyes of the people of Mnemosyne. They can't afford to let you go on as you have every time you're permitted freedom to speak—spreading your malicious lies and half-truths about the new order. So they are graciously giving you a second chance. Either you accept the post and adhere to the vow of secrecy that an Orrery commandant must take—or else suffer the consequences."

"I see," Doyle said, smiling wanly, glancing from Petra to Kagan. "And I also see that there *is* something between the two of you after all."

Petra was defiant. Her eyes blazed. "Yes!" she cried. "You see correctly!"

"Petra!" Kagan started.

She waved him back. "It isn't any use. He deserves the whole truth." She paused and looked up at Doyle, biting her lip, her gaze now fawning. "I wanted to spare you this, but I've no choice. You'd find out sooner or later. Kagan has proposed, and I told him I'd think it over."

"I see."

She fell silent for a moment. After glancing once again at Kagan, she said to Doyle, "Does this change what you agreed—that you'd accept the Orrery post?"

Doyle smiled thinly. "Should it?"

For a moment she was at a loss for words. She nodded. "No. Of course not."

Kagan stepped forward, hand extended. "Friends?" he asked Doyle.

Doyle shook his hand. Then he stepped back and said, a quality of authority in his tone, "Kagan, as my first officer-to-be, I think it would be unwise for us to let our personal differences interfere with our duties."

"You're right, Doyle. I'll see that they don't."

Doyle smiled at Petra. "Whatever your decision, I wish you my best." He turned and started to leave, but Kagan called to him.

"Just a moment. At 0400 this afternoon I'm to escort you to the great hall of the Justivac where you are to have an audience before the supreme council. There you will be examined and questioned at length concerning your allegiance to the new order. If they find you acceptable, you are to be billeted in the commandant's quarters at the Orrery, and then you will be presented to the staff. I shall personally conduct you on a tour of the Orrery and acquaint you with the operations and what your responsibilities are to be."

"I have a vague idea of what an Orrery commandant is expected to do."

"Beg pardon, Captain Doyle," Kagan said curtly, "but it's been a long time since you've been here in Mnemosyne and a great many changes have been made. The operations of an Orrery complex are different from what they were back in the old days."

"The old days . . ." Doyle smiled.

Kagan looked at him but did not see the humor of it. He was grim as he continued, "Once you are indoctrinated, there will be no return to the frontier and no freedom to speak your mind. Is that clear? You will have to take the oath of secrecy."

Doyle nodded. "A most effective way to silence men like me," he said with a touch of bitterness.

"Yes," Kagan said without smiling. "Now if you'll come along with me, there's just enough time to catch the ceremonies at the statue of Cleo before our appointment at the hall."

Just as Doyle fell into step beside Kagan, a man darted out

37

of the foliage at the edge of the path and swung an object at Kagan's head. Kagan groaned and sunk to the pavement. Doyle instinctively lurched around and lunged at the attacker. The man threw up his hands and whispered, "Captain Doyle! *Don't*, I'm a friend."

Doyle halted. He stared at the man, wondering where he had seen him before. He decided to say nothing.

"There are many of us who think and believe as you," the man said. "Others believe you have joined the order of the Secretariat. I hope to God you haven't. How say you?"

Doyle was suspicious. "I say as I always have said. I don't go for the new order and what they stand for. I don't agree that we ought to enslave ourselves to a machine."

There was a flicker of relief in the man's eyes as he smiled and said, "Forgive me this way of getting word to you. It was the only way. Kagan is not to be trusted. We wanted you to know there is an underground, and we are organizing now to fight the new order. Are you with us?"

Doyle nodded slowly. "Yes. I'm gratified to know I'm not alone. Who are your leaders?"

The man retreated suddenly, drawing to the side of the path in the cover of the plants. "We will contact you again. Go along with the Secretariat. But be careful. They will probe your mind, search the very depths of your soul. It won't be easy to fool them. Do you understand?"

Doyle nodded. There was a groan from Kagan on the ground. He glanced at him and when he looked up again, the man had vanished.

Kagan sat up, holding the back of his head. "What happened?"

"I don't know," Doyle said. "I think it might have been meant for me. One of your insurgents, no doubt. Are you all right?"

"As good as can be expected," Kagan said, arising, looking around, his eyes seething with anger.

4

Justivac

The aide stood aside and touched the disc around his neck, which activated the chamber door, permitting Doyle to enter the vast hall through the security screen.

"Proceed to the keystone in the center beneath the dome and stand easy, Captain Doyle," a page told him when he entered. "Place both your feet on the concordance markings and concentrate on the first hundred rooms of the mnemonic code. Before long you will be audited by the Secretariat."

Doyle did as he had been instructed. He gingerly entered the hall, and the door slid shut with a metallic clang behind him, sealing him in. His footsteps echoed as he walked toward the glowing keystone in the center of the glazed floor. He closed his eyes briefly and purged from his mind the memories of the revolutionary he had met that day. He knew it would be perilous if such thoughts were in his mind when he stepped upon the stone. He would need to purge his mind of all responses except those that would be acceptable to the Justivac. If a memory of a man who had attacked Kagan or of the others who had shown such intense dislike for him during the honor assembly on the plaza entered his mind and caused a physiological or psychological change in him, he would be doomed.

He looked up and saw, high above, a shimmering, cycling spheroid of light that appeared to pulsate with a slow regularity.

Although Doyle had never been inside the chamber before, he had heard enough about it during the years since the Secretariat had come to power that he felt not at all strange. He knew he would be challenged and asked to display his ability to assimilate mems of knowledge at ten-second intervals. Ever since he had first aspired to master the mind code back on earth some twenty years before, when he had entered the secret compound deep in the Rocky Mountains in the United States and had qualifed to enter the training center preparatory to joining the first colony ship that was subsequently launched to Pulsar 143, he had dutifully used the mnemonic code daily. It had assisted him in his tasks, amused him, whiled away the monotonous time whenever the routine of duty pressed inward on him, and helped him put from his mind the longing he had felt for Petra during the lonely months of duty in the desolate plains and on the forbidden frontiers of the planet. He lived and breathed the mnemonic code and through its myriad facets he delved into the sources of all the knowledge and memories he had assimilated during his lifetime. He welcomed the examination and the challenge it represented. He was eager to begin—to prove that his mind could not be tapped or made controllable by fear of the Justivac.

As soon as he stepped onto the keystone and looked down at the ancient markings of the hundred places within the room of his mind, he became aware of a sound vibrating all around him, pulsating in rhythm to the alpha wave pattern of his brain.

He blocked from memory all traces of his recent encounters and thought instead of the markings on the floor that matched the memory rooms in the library of his mind.

Slowly at first he recalled the symbols that represented the mental storage shelves for the orderly filing of memory bits. He saw the images like great walls through which he journeyed in memory. All things merged together as he traveled back in time, and each symbol represented a chain of knowledge and experience linked with other chains. On the first corridor of memory he gazed down at the floor and saw from left to right nine boxes in three rows. The odd corners had odd numbers. In the center was number five. Good old number five, he thought and was amused. It was important to be amused, and relaxed. The machine attuned to the nervous system, and the slightest variation from the norm would cause it to scrutinize him relentlessly.

He saw in his mind's eye the numbers no longer abstract, but concrete, as objects he could peg his memories on. Faster and faster he concentrated on recalling the numbers. He fixed his memory powers on whole walls at a time and then could envisage fifty and then one hundred places at once. He stood transfixed, unaware of the passage of time.

"Captain Doyle, you have done well."

Doyle opened his eyes and gazed upward. The cycling spheroid of pulsing light in the dome overhead descended. He did not dare to relax his vigil. He kept his thoughts to remain on the mind code.

A voice whirred like the wings of a thousand birds in flight. "You are honored here Doyle, number fifteen of Pioneeer Force One, because you have served faithfully and diligently all the years you have been on Pulsar 143 and because you have distinguished yourself by destroying the alien invaders who would have conquered us had they been allowed to establish a base here. It is now the Secretariat's privilege to bid you welcome to the briefing. You have been cleared through security.

"As one who has been nominated for the post of Orrery commandant, you will fix your mind on what is about to be transmitted to you in the usual manner. Once you have been

41

programmed, you will be committed, under pain of death, to guard these secrets until the end of your days. Is that understood, Captain Doyle?"

Doyle murmured, "Yes. I hear and I understand. I will guard these secrets with my life. I will program them into my mind and will forever hold them sacred, only to be used in the performance of my duty."

He had said the correct thing. It was standard protocol. He had learned the technique long before he had arrived on the planet, and he knew that this formality had not been altered, though all other things were. He forced his mind to remain on the subject at hand. He knew the Justivac was still monitoring his responses and the slightest rise in respiration or nervous response would trigger it to examine him as it might a criminal or a traitor to the cause.

"Very good, Captain Doyle. Now, you are herewith put on notice that you are, as of the moment the briefing begins, *un*free. You will no longer function as a free spirit in this or any other community on this planet. Is that clear? Do you have any misgivings? Do you wish, for any reason, to withdraw yourself from this nomination? Speak now or forever remain silent."

"I have no misgivings. I have no reason to withdraw myself from the nomination."

"A note of hesitancy is detected in your graph," the voice from above said. "Do you care to explain?"

"Yes," Doyle said quickly, realizing that for a moment he had thought of his feelings about the injustice the Secretariat had invoked on the colonists by making everyone obey the Justivac and live by its three estates. He said quickly, "I shall miss my freedom as commander of the pioneer force Tangier. I shall miss the adventure of exploring new horizons for my people. That is why I hesitated."

There was a long pause as the whirring overhead decreased. Finally it increased again and the voice said, "You shall not

42

regret having been promoted. The duties of Orrery commandant are far more diverse, interesting, and complex. You shall not have time to reflect upon your past, and this is good."

"Yes," Doyle said woodenly, "it is good."

"We have observed you during the past years of the rise of the new order, and we have recorded your efforts to induce others to voice their objections against the government. You have failed in this endeavor as we knew you would. You were one man against many. What is more, you learned that people wish to be governed rather than do the governing themselves. Is not the fact of their apathy evidence of this?"

"Yes, I will agree the citizens show little interest in having a voice in their government."

"Despite your contrary nature—or shall we term it *rebellious?*—we have decided you are the most deserving man on Pulsar 143 for the post of Orrery commandant. From now on you will be required to keep your views and opinions to yourself. Is that clear?"

"Yes, perfectly," Doyle said.

"The Secretariat will require your allegiance to the new order. Can it be counted upon?"

"Yes," Doyle said, gazing up at the spheroid.

"We have judged you to be a dependable man—one who is dedicated to the code. We know this because of your past record, Captain Doyle. Now, before the programming of your mind begins, do you wish to speak?"

Knowing what was expected of him, Doyle said, "I pledge my loyalty to the new order, and I accept the responsibility of keeping in trust the secrets programmed into my brain. I herewith pledge that I shall nevermore speak out against the regime, nor will I incite others to do so. From this day on I shall not in any way speak of overthrowing the Secretariat and the new order."

"We are pleased by your attitude," the spheroid replied.

Doyle almost smiled to himself. He had just pledged that he

would never speak out against the regime; he had not said a word about *acting* against it. He had not taken an oath falsely.

But he was wary. He decided to establish himself as a citizen who had acted in accordance with the dictates of his character. He did not want to leave something unsaid that might later be cause for the Secretariat to recall him for interrogation. He clasped his hands behind his back and looked up. "There *is* something else I should like to discuss before the programming begins."

"Speak."

"Am I to understand that you have selected me because of my qualifications and experience and not because of the wish to silence me?"

"You understand correctly."

"But once I accept the post and am briefed and programmed, I will no longer be permitted the freedom of speech? I shall henceforth be required to maintain silence to affirm my eternal allegiance?"

"Yes, that too is correct. You are to be entrusted with the responsibility of keeping state secrets so sacred that only death will relieve you of this obligation."

"What about Petra—and the man who is to be my first officer, the man called Kagan?"

"Ah, yes, 914 and 772, the daughter of 913 and the son of 771. Both loyal and true subjects. *Chamberists.*"

"*Chamberists?*" frowned Doyle, indicating that he was not familiar with the term.

"Yes, Chamberists. They are charged with the duty of maintaining security. Before you were directed to this chamber for this examination and briefing, they were the ones who cleared your dossier with the Justivac. Had they not had confidence in you and your ability to administrate the duties of Orrery commandant, they would not have cleared your dossier. They have stated that your outspokenness of past years was nothing more than the idle griping of an individualist type. You are the last of your breed, Doyle. We give thanks for that. It behooves us now to state that Petra and Kagan have placed their lives in jeopardy on your behalf. Should you prove to be a security risk, they will be phased out with you. Is that clear?"

"I understand." It took some effort for him to control himself. He said no more.

"Are you ready to begin the programming, Captain Doyle?"

"Yes." He held his hands loosely behind him, fingers relaxed, so as not to cause his palms to perspire. The Justivac's sensors were able to detect the slightest physiological or psychological change in any living body. He knew that one bead of perspiration would be enough to cause it to subject him to one of the most arduous tests ever devised—a test few had ever walked away from without being reduced to the state of a servoman.

The only way to emerge victorious from this contest with the electronic brain was through concentration on the mnemonic code. He fixed his thoughts on the repository wall in the first room in his memory, and then on each succeeding decade of walls. The images in his memory grew large and brilliant and sharply in focus. He saw them, could reach out and touch them; then he separated himself and entered each of the compartments in which his memories were stored, touching each place in turn, bodily, physically, mentally.

It was a superhuman feat of concentration that only a few among the many thousands who had colonized the planet had managed.

The programming began. At ten-second intervals the duties were called. He did not think of what he was being instructed to do; instead, he concentrated merely on assimilating each instruction without regard to how he was to employ it when the time came.

"Orrery programmed to alter basic human brain nuclei."

He assimilated this with the first box in the second decade.

"Orrery activated to alter human brain nuclei in stages by depressing series B switches."

Doyle deposited this in the second box in the second decade of his memory bank. He dared not consider the horror of what he was assimilating or the mighty power that would be his to administer. He dared not think of the diabolical use for which the Orrery had been subverted. The Secretariat had devised the complex for the purpose of controlling the minds of the citizens of Pulsar 143. Doyle forced himself with every erg of energy he could muster *not* to consider the terrible thing the Secretariat had done. He realized this was part of the test—that the Secretariat had hoped he would react like a rebel—but he was determined to succeed.

He concentrated on the mems being committed to memory. He concentrated on keeping in tune with the callings. He remained utterly devoid of emotion. The slightest alteration of his mental state would mean death!

The instruction continued.

Doyle, eyes closed again, concentrated on the briefing without thought to his wearying body, his tired legs, or the fact that the rhythmic callouts had exceeded the two-hundredth mental file chamber limit. On and on it went, until the number four hundred eighty-five. It was over.

The briefing was complete. His brain was programmed. But his rationale was unscathed. He had not been brainwashed. He had merely soaked up the teaching like a sponge.

Revolution was in the air. There was an underground. And he would be a part of it. It was for this reason that he pretended to go along. It was for this reason that he allowed them to indoctrinate him—to enslave him—to burden his mind.

"Recitation, please. In reverse order."

With a smile of relief, Doyle shifted his legs and stretched. He unclasped his hands behind him, stretched his fingers and reclasped his hands. Then he began the recitation, calling out in reverse order all the instructions that had been programmed into his mind.

When the task was done without a single error—the cycling spheroid descended until it was but a few inches over him. "Congratulations, *Commandant* Doyle. You are now in possession of the complete concordance that renders you capable of administering the operation of the Orrery complex. Retire now to your new quarters and contemplate all that you have just assimilated. Under pain of death you will neither forget nor utter to another living soul all that you have just mastered here on this historic day."

Doyle bowed and stepped down from the concordance keystone. The cycling spheroid whirled up and vanished. Abruptly the throbbing sensation stopped, and he felt an oppressive silent vacuum surround him. As he walked toward the door and heard the sounds of his shoes on the glazed floor, his mind cleared and he was able to depart from the recesses of his mind. The door opened to let him pass through.

Once outside in the conditioned atmosphere, he felt a strong sense of accomplishment and of relief. But this was short-lived. Two aides attired in burnished gold military uniforms complete with tranquilizer cyclonders at their sides fell into step on either side of him and escorted him to the test vestibule.

As soon as they were inside the cab, the doors folded, and they were fired like missiles through the bowels of the city. Within a few seconds they were deep inside the Orrery Citadel high above the weathersphere. A minute later the aides were escorting him to his quarters. They snapped to attention at either side of the doorway.

Doyle told them to stand easy. Slowly he walked inside and looked around. His new quarters were far more sumptuous than any he had seen since he had left earth. He had had no idea that a commandant was granted such a luxurious apartment.

It reminded Doyle of the way the earth governments treated their high officials, statesmen, and military governors, and he did not like it. He saw no need for elaborately furnished living quarters. He had learned to live with functional things rather than articles created simply for decoration. He wondered why the Secretariat had departed from their concepts of old and regressed to the materialistic practices so common to earth. They were on Pulsar 143, not on earth, and this fact alone made him uncomfortable when looking at his ornate surroundings. It was almost as though the Secretariat had known it would displease him rather than flatter his ego, and he strongly resented it. Why should he luxuriate in such splendor when everyone else on the planet was content to live the simple life?

He wondered how it had happened that the Secretariat had selected him for a position of such power—unless it was to place him in a post where he could be watched constantly and where he could be silenced—or controlled. This disturbed Doyle, but he decided not to waste time thinking about it. There were other more important things to consider—like what he ought to do to organize the dissidents on the planet.

He sat in the chair facing the cityview screen and touched the button. At once a panoramic three-dimensional scene of Mnemosyne came into focus. There was no corner of the city he could not see. Concealed cameras were everywhere, and he was surprised at how well they were camouflaged. He studied the nomenclature on the miniature hand console beside the chair and learned that he could view at will any corner within the city limits, including most of the gardens and all of the paths of the muses within the labyrinth. For a moment he was almost overwhelmed by the power at his fingertips. Then he became pensive and morose. He reviewed mentally all that he had assimilated during the hours he had spent on the concordance keystone, and he felt sick because of it.

As Orrery commandant he would be answerable to the

Secretariat and would also be the Justivac's number one lackey. Originally, an Orrery was used to keep a record of the heavenly bodies in orbit; but the Secretariat had subverted it for their own purposes.

It dawned on Doyle with the impact of a physical blow that he could be held personally responsible for the safety and security of every living soul on the planet. Moreover, he would actually have access to the control consoles at the very heart of the complex. It frightened him to think that any one man could have so much power. It was for this very reason that their group had left the earth to colonize Pulsar 143.

Now he was right back where he had started from.

The Orrery system consisted of a highly complex force field that could manipulate every living being on the planet when and if activated. It could cause neighbor to turn against neighbor, or cause parents to turn against children as though all were mortal enemies.

The system had been put together while he had been in the field with the pioneer forces. He had had no idea that the new order had gone so far and now he understood why it had become necessary for the Secretariat to utilize a government format under the Justivac's rule. The entire thing was too vast for any group of men to administer.

Doyle found himself totally incredulous. It did not seem plausible to him that he had been made commandant of such a complex. Then it hit him—he could very well be the scapegoat, the fall guy. If the power of the Orrery was subverted for evil purposes, he would be blamed.

Of course! They had delivered him to the people as a hero. They would continue to do so until he was elevated to a position of national esteem. Then they would lower the boom. The Secretariat would activate the Orrery, reduce the people to the condition of servopeople, and hold him responsible. After that, it would be too late. There would be no place on that planet for him to go—and the Secretariat would push the

Justivac's buttons, which would in turn operate the Orrery complex.

He reviewed all that he had been programmed to learn. As he reviewed, he intellectualized and began to make sense of the facts and their diabolical order. Boden, the father of Bodmew, was number 912. Bodmew was 913, and Petra was 914. Petra's grandfather had been the first Orrery commandant!

These facts suddenly began to reveal something to Doyle. Could it be possible that Petra, and possibly Kagan as well, *knew* something of the enormity of the project—and what was in store for him once he officially took the post—the same post that her grandfather had commanded for so many years?

For the moment Doyle considered only Petra's role. She had played-it well. She had not given him an inkling as to what would be expected of him once he took over the Orrery command.

Doyle knew he had a responsibility of such awesome magnitude that neither he nor any other human being, machine, computer, or servoman, was capable of handling it.

Instinctively he felt that Petra had risked her life to get him in this post—but he could not be sure. If she had risked all, was it because she knew and understood the terrible power the Orrery complex was capable of exercising over the planet's settlers? And, if this was so, did she want him to destroy the Orrery and its potential—or perhaps to do something about stopping others from gaining control of it?

No matter what, Doyle decided he would act according to the dictates of his conscience.

Man had journeyed from earth in 2082 and 2083 with the noble purpose of colonizing other planets. But he had only succeeded in establishing a colony on Pulsar 143. The other missions had aborted.

Shortly after Doyle's group had established a colony on the planet, the mind code was adopted and the City of

50

Mnemosyne founded. Ever since, the people had prospered. Men like Doyle had slaked their thirst for adventure by exploring the desolate frontiers that lay beyond the settlement. For seventeen years, Doyle and others like him had occupied themselves with the task of exploring, while others *un*like him occupied themselves with the task of rising to power.

He had been away too long. His chronological age, like that of most others of the original colony was a mere 1.7 percent that of their descendants. For those born on Pulsar 143, more than a century had elapsed and three generations had risen—but now he would need to do some catching up. He wondered if it was too late.

Was Mnemonsyne to crumble into the dust because a new order had been established? What should he do? That question nettled Doyle to the very marrow of his bones. For now, all he could do was bide his time and try to find old Boden's plans—which he was certain were concealed somewhere in the Orrery complex.

With a slight smile tugging at the corners of his mouth, Doyle touched the emblem on his communicator ring and summoned his servostaff.

"Come here at once. I wish to program you for your duties."

If only he could program himself too.

5

Sanctus Sanctum

After three days and nights in the Orrery commandant's quarters Doyle was no closer to the solution he had been seeking than he was when he had first arrived there.

Why had he been promoted to Orrery commandant?

He was still unsure of the real reason.

However he was confident of one thing. It *had* been Petra who had engineered his appointment. No other explanation was plausible. Of the original fifteen captains who preceded Doyle in seniority and who were still alive and on active duty with the pioneer force, twelve were more qualified than he for the appointment and the others were on a par with him. Yet somehow Petra had managed to have him placed ahead of his colleagues. How she had managed to bypass them he had no idea. He was convinced that his defeat of the alien invading forces had had little or nothing to do with it. According to the constitution the Secretariat was not empowered to grant appointments to officers merely because they were popular or because they had accomplished something above and beyond the call of duty.

If Petra had managed this alone, it was certainly no small effort on her part. He wondered what she had had to do in order to have him placed in such a post. On the other hand, if she had not done it alone, who had helped her?

Kagan?

Out of the question.

Doyle decided he needed time to find the answers. He could not risk anything until he knew which way to move and with whom he could secretly ally himself. He could hardly expect to do it alone. He was certain of one thing: the Orrery complex had to be destroyed at any cost.

As commandant he was free to come and go as he wished, but always in the company of the two aides—the uniformed armed guards who had been with him from the moment he left the great hall.

During his three days on the new post Doyle had had only one brief meeting with Kagan. Although he had wanted to spend more time with Kagan to get to know him better and to orient himself with the complex workings of the Orrery, he had not pressed the issue because he did not wish to make Kagan suspicious of him. It would have been an error to give him the impression that he had done a sudden turnabout and was anxious to get busy with the duties he had not wished to assume in the first place. He knew it was unwise to underestimate Kagan. If anything he was a dangerous man in a very high place and he would bear watching.

Doyle decided to treat Kagan with respect and to remember always that he was his second in command, his first officer, and not consider him a friend or even Petra's fiancé. He decided to treat him as a technician and a man of consequence.

The original intent of the settlers on Pulsar 143 was to eliminate the competitive system that had wrought havoc on earth. They were successful at first—and then the new order had taken over while Doyle was on duty on the frontier. How this had taken place and how the duly elected colonists had been overthrown, Doyle did not understand. No explanations had been sent to him on the other side of the planet. Word reached him that imperfect man had replaced his leaders with the perfect machine—the Justivac. The new order was established and twenty-six citizens were made secret members of the Secretariat.

Doyle had explored his quarters—Boden's former quarters—many times in search of clues but had been unable to turn up anything. He felt confident however that somewhere within those quarters were clues to what Boden's plans had been. If such clues did exist, Doyle knew they would be so subtle and inconspicuous that they would be certain to be overlooked by searchers. He put himself in Boden's place. He knew enough about the old man to accurately guess at his mental frame, his character, and most of all, his inherent sense of responsibility to his fellow man. Doyle knew that Boden would not have willingly supervised the building of the Orrery and then see it put to such a diabolical use unless he had been forced to do so. With this understanding of Boden, Doyle was sure that he would find what he was searching for.

Doyle did not doubt for one moment that the quarters were searched periodically as well as monitored continuously with highly sophisticated surveillance gear. He had the eerie feeling that he was living every moment under glass, the object of scrutiny, no doubt by the twenty-six pairs of eyes of the Secretariat.

The Secretariat had entrusted him with the task of containing or commanding the routine operation of the Orrery; but they did not trust him enough to come and go without being under the watchful eyes of the guards.

He sat idly before the viewer, watching the comings and goings of the populace, wondering if they were aware they were being spied upon too. He decided they did not know. As the viewer scanned the streets and malls of the inner city near the amphitheater, he caught a glimpse of Petra emerging from the gate. He sat forward and activated his communicator ring. Faintly resounding tones could be heard as he pressed 914.

He saw her pause and move to one side of the crowded

walk to be out of the way of the people hurrying away from the amphitheater after the evening concert that had just ended. It had been a highly spirited performance of Tschaikovsky's Swan Lake.

"Did you enjoy the ballet?" he asked when he saw she had pressed the receive module.

"Oh, it's you, Doyle. Yes, I did very much. Did you watch it?"

"For a few minutes on my viewer."

"How are you getting on, Commandant?"

There was a touch of something he could not define in her tone. "No complaints," he said. "I just happened to see you, and I got the urge to say hello."

"You're watching me . ... ?" she asked, glancing around and smiling, a bit amused because she could not locate the hidden video camera.

"Yes. How about having dinner with me?"

"Now?"

"Yes. I miss you, Petra. I'd like to talk to you . . . to sort of make amends."

She tossed her head in that girlish way of hers that he recalled with a twinge of nostalgia that made him feel the weight of his years quite suddenly. "Don't refuse me, Petra. I'm sorry for antagonizing you before—"

"You did no such thing. I understand. It all came like a thunderbolt—unexpectedly. I know you never liked surprises. It was my fault. I deserved that. I should've remembered from the old days that you lead an orderly, planned life and you detest being placed at a disadvantage."

"We'll talk about it over dinner," he said. "I respectfully request the pleasure of your company and your charming companionship for dinner. Is that formal enough? I remember from the old days," he added with a terse laugh, "that you always liked things polite and formal."

He watched her on the viewer for a moment. She caught

herself and frowned slightly, then she smiled. It was as though she had noticed that he had just asked her very subtly to help him. She recalled that only twice during all the years they had known each other had Doyle ever deigned to address her in that fashion.

Of course those two occasions were hardly to be construed as being as formally voiced as this one. She knew Doyle better than she knew anyone else on Pulsar 143. She knew he wanted her now, and she acknowledged that she had received his veiled message loud and clear.

"I shan't refuse you, Doyle," she said. "I'll be up in a few minutes. Have cocktails waiting, darling."

"The usual?" he asked.

"Why, of course," she said without hesitation. Her reply conveyed that she knew and understood what he wanted. Neither Doyle nor Petra had ever had a cocktail together that they could have referred to as being "usual." It was in this way that they understood and acknowledged what was on their minds.

A few minutes after Petra had arrived and they were seated in the enormous living room overlooking the eastern frontier and the six red roons glowing in the far horizon, Doyle toasted her with his goblet. Then he frowned. Through pursed lips he spoke as though unaware of the eyes and ears watching them. "Petra, my dear," he began stiffly, again conveying the hidden intent in his words, "how long have we known each other?"

"Why do you ask?"

He smiled and toyed with his goblet. He shrugged. "It seems like forever, doesn't it? But tell me, how long has it been?"

"Years and years. We were childhood sweethearts, remember? Surely you haven't forgotten?"

"No, of course not. But I wouldn't say we were sweethearts. Aside from carrying your books home occasionally, I was no more to you than Kagan or any of the others."

She blinked at him. She got the message. "Yes," she said with a silky smile, "I suppose you're right. But why do you ask? You sound so authoritarian—so aloof."

Doyle did not smile. He was pleased because she was getting the message. It would not do for the Secretariat to think she had recommended him for the post because of their relationship either past or present. "You may think me rather presumptuous, but I have a question I must ask you."

"Ask away, Commandant Doyle."

He arose and clasped his hands behind his back. He paced the floor several times, halted, then rocked back and forth on his heels. "I've thought this over carefully, Petra, so please don't for a moment misconstrue what I'm about to say."

"Dear Doyle," she broke impatiently, "make your point. You're exhausting me with this suspense."

He laughed. "Okay, I'd like to make a formal request of the Secretariat that you be relieved of your present duties and reassigned to me—as my assistant."

She sat forward. "Why *me*—of all people?" She sat staring, mouth open, eyes glinting with amusement and wonder.

"Because you grew up here in the Orrery—didn't you?"

"How did you guess?"

The smile that came to Doyle's face was smug. "The geophysicist who established the Orrery preceded you in number by two digits. He was 912. Boden—your grandfather. Wasn't he?"

She bowed her head and sighed. He felt she had sighed in relief and had tried to convey this to him. "Yes, he was."

"When your father, Bodmew, was placed in command of the transient citadel, you left him to come here to live with your grandfather. Am I correct?"

"How did you know that?"

He turned up his hands. "It was elementary. The transient citadel is no place for children, so your father had to send you to live here. If I were he, I would have done the same thing.

Since your grandfather had so much to offer you, it was only natural that he take you in and take care of you." Doyle paused and smiled. "And if you grew up in this place, certainly you know a great deal more about it than I—or even Kagan or the good gentlemen of the Secretariat. Am I correct?"

"Quite," she said with a smile. "Then you have not located the Sanctus Sanctum either?"

"The *what?*"

"My grandfather's study. It was alleged to be here—in some secret place. No one has ever been able to find it. After he died they searched and searched, but it never could be found." She looked at him, her eyes hard. It was as though she were trying to tell him not to answer the question she was about to ask. Then she wet her lips with the tip of her tongue and said, "You haven't located it, have you?"

"No. I didn't even know such a room existed."

"It isn't supposed to be a room—exactly. It's more like a secret hiding place where he used to keep his notes and do his research. I can't tell you more than that, Doyle. I don't know any more myself. I'm under oath to the Secretariat never to betray any state secrets unless I am so ordered. Therefore, even if I knew of the existence of this secret room, I would be duty bound not to tell you. Make your formal request and if they approve, I shall be delighted to be your assistant." Her voice uttered the words, but he knew from her intonation that she was telling him she had to ask the question—and also to warn him not to reveal the location of the hidden study if he should discover it.

"And what about Kagan?" he asked, pretending concern.

"What about him?" she came back, smiling, her eyes wide open, glittering.

Doyle shrugged. This was neither the time nor the place to discuss Kagan. There would be time enough for that later. He went to her as she arose and escorted her to the door. Then he kissed her on the cheek. The door opened and a servomaid appeared. She smiled at Petra, curtsied, and said, "It is good to see you, mistress. See, I still curtsy as you taught us."

Petra laughed. She looked at Doyle, explaining, "This is Nanny. She was my Nanny a long time ago when I was a little girl. Grandpa taught me to curtsy, and I taught her and the other servomaids." ·

Doyle studied the servomaid's serene and youthful face. She looked no more than twenty-two. "You were one of the first here on 143, weren't you? Nanny transposed into the numerical code is 22."

"Yes, Commandant Doyle, sir," the servomaid said. "Before I was salvaged and transported from earth I was a victim of Down's Syndrome. I was a hopeless case. But in the transport lab I was transfigured, and now I am a useful servomaid. I am happy to be a servomaid." Her voice sounded mechanical, almost artificial, almost unpleasant. "I live only to serve. I am Nanny, number twenty-two."

"That's enough, Nanny," Petra said.

"I am pleased, I am pleased to be a servomaid," the transfigured girl went on.

"I said, that's enough!" Petra said sharply.

The servomaid smiled and fell silent. She curtsied again and turned and went down the corridor. When she was gone, Petra touched Doyle's arm. "I'll let you know as soon as I've been audited by the Secretariat. Perhaps I might be able to help you find grandfather's Sanctus Sanctum—if it's really here."

Going out, Petra laughed. It was a cryptic laugh, one calculated to make Doyle think. As he watched the door close after her, it suddenly occurred to him that all the while they had been together Petra had been acting stiffly formal, as though she had wanted to convey something to him but had not dared to because of the audiovisual surveillance. Then it began to break in his mind like the dawn of a new day. *Sanctus Sanctum.* The words were the key! Transposed into numerals 02710 02713, then retransposed into phonetic language the vowels as usual not counting, but used only to formulate the consonants into numerical equivalents, he phrased under his breath the words, "sink toes—sink time."

He yawned and stretched and retired to the bathroom. He began to undress, and then he closed the door and turned on the steam bath so the room flooded with swirling clouds of vapor. When the mirrors and glazed surfaces were heavily fogged, he dropped to his knees at the foot of the sink and explored the tubular construction, paying close attention to every detail.

After several minutes he discovered the secret. At the base of the piping was a small nodule the size of a pea. It appeared to be little more than a flaw in the tubing. He pressed it and at once the sink began to rise. A compartment large enough to accommodate a man was revealed behind it. At last he had broken the code and found the elusive secret compartment that Petra's grandfather had so cleverly concealed in the quarters. He knew the steam had sufficiently fogged the surveillance cameras to allow him to work in secret. He crawled though the panel and found himself inside a small room lined with neat rows of notebooks and curious control boxes and panels. No wonder the Secretariat knew nothing of the inner sanctum. Who could find it? Its clever concealment attested to the ingenuity of Petra's grandfather. Only a brilliant mind like his could have conceived of such a device to hide his secrets from the prying eyes of the Secretariat. Who would suspect the presence of such a compartment right under the watchful lenses of the scanners?

And what of 02713? Sanctum—*sink time.* What did *sink time* mean? Doyle looked around. After several minutes of searching he found it—a clock. It was affixed to the rear of the bathroom fixture. He examined it carefully and drew a sharp breath in surprise when he realized it was an atomic clock. The central portion was not activated. A red seal was placed over the release mechanism. Upon the seal were the numbers

121450250590501. Doyle chewed his bottom lip anxiously as he transposed the numerals into consonants and then the consonants into words. He formed the vowel sounds and heard only the numerical values of the consonants: 121—don't . . . 450—release . . . 250—unless!

Perspiration began to ooze freely from his face as he continued the mnemonic transposition: 5—all . . . 9—hope . . . 0—is . . . 501—lost!

There it was! The old man had constructed a built-in self-destruct mechanism.

His hand recoiled from the clock. He mopped his brow and glanced about at the rows of notebooks and other items. Then crawled backward through the opening, touched the node on the pipe, and watched the swingaway sink fixture return to place against the wall.

He arose, undressed, and stepped into the steam bath. Now he knew. Now he understood that Petra had known all along and was awaiting the chance to help him. But to help do *what?* Was she pledged to the Secretariat and was she interested only in learning the location of the hidden room? Or was she against the Secretariat and interested in overthrowing them? He could not believe this—her actions had indicated she was loyal to the Secretariat.

So far he had not been shown through the Orrery complex. And so far, Kagan had put off every opportunity to escort him through the system.

As Doyle was cooling off beneath a refreshing shower, he began to smile to himself as an idea came to mind. It was amusing in its simplicity. But would it work?

He thought about the time in the scheme of things on Pulsar 143. He had been there for seventeen years, but for Petra and the others, it had been years and years. When then did time move more slowly for him and more rapidly for the others?

Of the original settlers to arrive on the planet, only a

handful remained—and they were all the same age as Doyle. He mulled this over and suddenly recalled something in a book he had once read. That book was called the Bible. In it was a story about a man called Abraham. Old Abraham purported to have lived to the ripe old age of 943. The numeral 943 was the equivalent of the name Abraham. Exactly *why* this occurred to him, Doyle did not know. The ancient Hebrews had no numerical digit system in their language, yet they were gifted in mathematics for the simple reason that they had perfected a better system—a mnemonic system in which all letters and words had meanings and numerical equivalents. In this manner the ancients could compute mathematically by *words*. This premise had been the basis for the mind code as adapted on the planet in the early days of the colony—but now it seemed to have been abandoned. This was all Doyle could think of to explain why the Secretariat had failed to find the location of the secret room simply by translating the words *Sanctus Sanctum* and then retransposing them into their real meaning: *sink toes—sink time.*

He wondered if he had walked into a trap—if the Secretariat were keeping him there merely to see what he would do when and if he found the sanctum. He decided to be wary of them and to watch his every step. Most of all he would have to watch Kagan and Petra until he knew exactly where they stood.

When he left the bath and sat before the viewer to watch the Secretariat's afternoon report to the people, he was unprepared for what he was about to witness. The spokesman for the Secretariat gravely informed the citizens of Pulsar 143 that beginning shortly, at a date and hour to be announced, all civil rights were suspended and certain other liberties were scheduled to be canceled.

The excuse given was that the Justivac was to be reprogrammed and such measures would be enforced only until the reprogramming was completed.

Doyle found this hard to believe. The Secretariat was moving faster than he had expected. Now he was certain of *why* they had installed him as Orrery commandant. He would be the perfect fall guy. He knew it would be announced later that he had been the one responsible for the new reforms of the new order. To be used in this fashion irked Doyle. He was frustrated and angry, and it was all he could do to contain his emotions. He switched off the viewer. Then he went to the great window and gazed out on the city. He could not bring his thoughts around to the Secretariat's way of thinking. He could not understand what they possibly had to gain by enslaving all the citizens on the planet. It did not make sense to him and it frightened him. On earth, this very thing had inspired the establishment of the first colony on this distant planet. Now earth history was being repeated on Pulsar 143.

What Doyle wondered about most was whether or not he would stand by and let it happen. What he wondered about least was what could he do about it—since he had discovered the existence of the atomic clock in the Orrery commandant's quarters. If the atomic clock were truly a self-destruct mechanism, he could put an end to the Secretariat and the Justivac and the Orrery too.

Then another thought struck him. What if the Secretariat *knew* that such a mechanism existed somewhere in the complex? Did this mean they intended for him to find it and then disarm it? Or did it mean they wanted him to lead them to it and then *they* would disarm it and hold it up as "evidence" that Commandant Doyle himself was the traitor and they had to invoke extreme measures against the populace until his plot was subverted?

The thought was terrifying.

Doyle knew now that no matter what he did, if he made one mistake, it could be the end of all civilization on Pulsar 143 as he and the other original settlers had meant it to be.

6

Ceremony

The servomaid drew back the window panels and Doyle's bedroom flooded with dazzling sunlight. The time was 0606 in the morning on his fifth day in the commandant's quarters on the top level of the Orrery complex.

Doyle's patience was at an end. He had been awake for hours, unable to relax in the sonic mufflers of the counterpane on his bed because his own inactivity and Kagan's strange dereliction of duty to him had brought him to the threshold of outrage. Though he fully realized this ploy was intended to push him into a state of nervousness and frustration, he could not rid himself of the outrage he felt. It was one thing to be appointed commandant, yet quite a different matter when that appointment proved to be a total farce. He knew now he had been given the post for several different reasons—all of which so far he had been unable to prove. His only hope lay with Kagan—but Kagan had been avoiding him like the plague. Every time he contacted Kagan, Kagan put him off.

His efforts to contact Petra met with failure too. And even when he had tried to contact his former commandant in the Pioneer Corps citadel, that too had been frustrated. He was now a virtual prisoner. Worse than this, during the past twenty-four hours his viewers, communicators, and other electronic equipment had been inoperative.

"Commandant Doyle," the clipped voice of one of his uniformed aides addressed him over the ceiling speakers, "First Officer Kagan has just arrived and respectfully requests permission to speak to you."

This amazed Doyle. Was this the thaw after the freeze? His first impulse was to leap out of his sontaic field bed and rush angrily into the other room to chew out his disobedient subordinate. But he knew this was just what the Secretariat wanted—evidence that he was unstable and given to temper tantrums. Or madness. He controlled the impulse and forced himself to laugh it off. He knew only too well that the new regime was trying to make him crack. He was stronger than they—he told himself—and he had to remind himself that he was going to continue to be stronger than they. Forcing himself to remain horizontal in the sontaic field bed, he stretched and yawned, feigning sleepiness. "Very well, I shall see him in a half hour. Have Kagan make himself at ease. I'll be out as soon as I've dressed and breakfasted."

"Yes, Commandant Doyle. Officer Kagan will wait. He has instructed me to send a uniform in to you. You are to wear this uniform."

"Uniform?" Doyle said, frowning and sitting up, watching one of the servomaids as she entered carrying a white tunic and trousers. She placed the clothing on the valet rack and then put a skull cap trimmed in gold braid on the dresser top. She stood to one side, gaze averted discreetly, head bowed, awaiting further orders.

Doyle got out of the bed and tightened the cinch on his briefs. He completed his toilette and then, saying nothing, he reached for the uniform and put it on. The servomaid came around behind him and soothed down the back of the tunic. He waved her away and strode across to the mirrored wall that housed the inoperative viewer, and he surveyed his appearance. He did not like it. The uniform was a bit too outlandish for his tastes. It was reminiscent of the imperialistic uniforms of the

Napoleonic era. He scowled at his reflection. The galley maid arrived with his breakfast and served it to him.

With calm deliberation Doyle took his breakfast, chewing the baked protein slowly, sipping the vegetea with almost imperceptible swallows. When he was finished, he arose and waited until the galley servomaid had cleared away the utensils and departed before he snapped his fingers at his female valet and motioned for her to help him on with his boots. He extended his right leg, then his left leg. The servomaid put the boots on him.

Doyle rose, dismissed her, and took his time placing his personal effects, handkerchief, pocket comb, vendor box key, pocket knife, unicard and emergency miniration energy sticks in his uniform pockets. The pocket knife and pocket rations he carried by force of habit.

Exactly thirty minutes had elapsed when he went through the automatic door and joined Kagan in the anteroom.

Kagan, who looked as though his patience had worn thin, was standing by the window shifting his weight from foot to foot. He turned and a forced smile came to his face. It was unusual to see a smile on Kagan's face. Doyle did not look pleased to see him.

Kagan was the empirical model of a professional soldier. His boots clicked smartly as he snapped to attention and saluted. "Good morning, sir. I trust your new uniform meets with your approval? It was specially tailored from the specifications on your dossier."

Doyle frowned. He glanced down at the tunic and the gold stripe along the outside seams of his snugly fitting trousers. "It does not please me. Wearing this kind of outlandish uniform is offensive. Since when do duty officers around here or any of the other citadels wear formal dress and braid for routine service?"

Kagan continued to hold his salute. He was waiting for Doyle to return the salute.

Doyle eyed him and said with a scoffing toss of his head, "For God's sake, Kagan, stop that nonsense. Put your hand down. I don't hold with militarism. I thought we left those rituals back on earth. But you wouldn't know that, would you? You were born here on 143."

Kagan reluctantly lowered his hand. The smile on his face faded in offense. He was slighted and he did not try to conceal it. In a deflated voice, he said, "I am here to escort you to the ceremony, sir." .

"*What* ceremony?"

Kagan was uneasy. He cleared his throat. "It's customary for the Secretariat to conduct a formal inaugural whenever a citadel commandant is invested."

"Pompous tomfoolery! Since when is *that* sort of thing the order of the day on this planet?" Doyle's eyes were narrowed in disdain. Undisguised revulsion was in his expression.

"Why should you be offended? What's so terrible about being formally inaugurated?"

"It smacks of the sort of thing that was wrong back on earth—the ridiculous ostentation and phony grandiloquence the militarists used to practice. That's just the thing that brought about the downfall of so many nations."

"I don't follow you. Surely, the nations on earth didn't fall just because of some rituals."

"The point is," said Doyle, "the countries and governments that condoned these practices nearly always collapsed. The common people saw in the pomp and ceremony of their governments an image they detested; so they were moved to overthrow them."

Almost defensively, but without apology, Kagan stammered, "I'm sorry you feel so strongly about that, Commandant Doyle. It isn't every day that a pioneer and hero of the people like you is awarded the highest technical command in this world for having saved us from the alien invasion fleet."

"All right, enough of your flattery. Let's get it over with."

Kagan dipped his head in acquiescence and gestured toward the door. Doyle led the way out. Kagan had to hurry to keep pace. They reached the transport tube and were stepping into the cab just as the two aides who had been at Doyle's side whenever he had left his chambers joined them. They saluted Doyle smartly.

Unaccustomed to the military formality, Doyle gave them a dispirited wave of his hand and a half-hearted smile and turned his attention up to the light panel inside the cab. Until that hour he had not even remotely guessed that the new order had gone so far as to incorporate the militaristic practices of the warlike governments he thought had been abandoned on earth. It nettled him to think that the Secretariat was leading the people back into old ways that were better off forgotten. For Doyle, militarism seemed a form of barbarism. Back on earth the build-up of such practices and formalities had always been the prelude to war, and he wondered if this might be happening here. Was history about to repeat itself on Pulsar 143? *Not if I can stop it,* thought Doyle. While working with the pioneer force, he had remained loyal to the dream that had inspired the colonization movement, and he had worked for the future of man on Pulsar 143. The sinking feeling that came over him then was due not to the abrupt descent in the transport—but rather to the feeling of impending danger, of the death and destruction that would be fostered by such regimentation.

He had heard that the new order had changed many things. What he learned of the function of the Orrery was bad enough, but the militarist regime and the accompanying pomp and ceremony, he failed to understand. He saw in all this the prelude to totalitarianism. From the pages of earth history Doyle recognized all the signs of history being repeated with all the mistakes of old included. The Secretariat was following in the footsteps of the militarist dictators, the Napoleons, the Hitlers, the Mussolinis, and the dozens of others who followed.

Doyle resolved then and there that he would die before he would see it happen all over again. Pulsar 143 was to have been man's first true Utopia. In the mnemonic code, 143 meant *dream*. Then suddenly it dawned on him that the number 143 also translated into the word *trauma*. It would surely become that if the Secretariat were allowed to get away with it. To get back his composure, Doyle thought through the code that had been perfected originally in 1843 by Francis Fauvel-Gouraud—the man who had amazed audiences on earth by demonstrating that man could tap the other 95 percent of his potential brain power by using his mind to develop a true photographic memory which he could use to the advantage of all mankind. The mind code had been adapted for the colonists long before the first expedition was launched. It had been put into use because at last man had learned how to use his intellect to the utmost and was now about to embark on greater adventures than ever before in his recorded history. Now the mind code was being abandoned. He wondered why. He wondered who was responsible.

Drawing a deep breath he repeated the mnemonic nomenclature, the *Ars Memoria*, the language of the mind. *T* and *D* sound alike. They stand for the numeral 1. Toe means one. Doe, tea, die—each means one. The vowels and *Y* do not count except to help form meaning out of consonants so words can be formed which enable the brain to remember numbers. Tidy, duty, date—stand for eleven.

When still a child, Doyle had learned the trick of reviewing the mental code. Now it relaxed him, stimulated his wit, enabled him to be rational whenever he was in danger or under stress.

Kagan touched Doyle's shoulder, awakening him from his dream state. "Commandant, sir. Will you please step this way?"

Doyle blinked and stepped out of the elevator cab. He and

Kagan walked briskly. They reached a doorway and the automatic panel slid inward to admit them.

They stepped onto the amphitheater stage and at once a loud fanfare from the orchestra at the front of the stage was heard, accompanied by a thunderous round of applause from the invisible audience beyond the lights.

Kagan stepped aside and with a gesture to Doyle, urged him to move to the center of the stage. "The spokesmen for the secretariat are in the wings to make the presentation and administer your oath of office. They are Abbot, Bailey, and Cecil—the three most highly placed officials in the government. For Petra's sake, Doyle, be civil to them, will you? She went way out in orbit for you, and if you should disgrace her after all she's done for you . . ."

Doyle ignored Kagan. He walked to the spotlighted center of the stage. The orchestra played a second fanfare and then a brief, rousing marching selection that Doyle could not quite place, though he had heard it before. The curtains behind the rostrum swung open, and three men in plain black tunics and knee-high boots rose from behind the speaker's platform and motioned to Doyle.

Beyond the lights at the foot of the stage, Doyle could now see the faces of the vast audience. It seemed the entire population had turned out for the occasion. As his eyes grew accustomed to the bright lights, he realized that the expressions on the faces of the people seemed somber, wooden—as though attending by obligation. There was not a vacant seat anywhere.

Doyle did not smile. He bowed stiffly, formally, but with some reluctance. He did not wish to bring Petra into disfavor so he did what was expected of him.

The trio stepped down to the center of the stage and the music ceased. Doyle recognized Abbott and was somewhat taken aback by his appearance. The last time he had seen Abbott, he was young and vigorous. But now he was old before his time. Doyle thought this most curious and a strong feeling of impending doom came over him when he recalled that Abbott had been one of the more liberal members of the government in the early days. Had they done this to him to silence him? It was Abbott who stepped before Doyle and hung the gleaming badge of the commandant's office around his neck. "With this symbol of authority we hereby invest in you, Commandant Doyle, the highest technical post on Pulsar 143. Now please repeat after me the oath of allegiance."

The words and the ceremony were meaningless to Doyle. Woodenly, he went through the motions of accepting the badge. He glimpsed Petra standing in the wings. She was smiling at him. However, her hands were clenched tightly at her sides, and when his gaze met hers, she averted her eyes to conceal from him the extent of her concern.

Doyle got it loud and clear. During that moment he realized that Petra was as hopelessly trapped as he.

After the inauguration and the brief commendation speeches by each of the Secretariat committeemen in which Doyle's exploits were enumerated for the benefit of the audience, the orchestra saluted him with a spirited rendition of Wagner's *Die Walküre*. Doyle was amused that they had selected the *Ride of the Valkyries* to play at his inauguration. The smile on his lips was not one of humble acceptance or gratitude.

Then Petra was ushered onto the stage and introduced. The audience was told that Petra, whose father was the commandant of the transient citadel, and whose grandfather had been the founder of the Orrery complex, was now officially appointed to serve as Doyle's assistant. The audience rose as if on command and gave them a standing ovation.

At last it was over, Doyle left the amphitheater with Petra at his side. They did not speak because of the risk of being overheard.

Not until they were in the elevator returning to the citadel did Petra speak for the first time. "I'll be honored to work with you, Commandant. I had no idea you had such a distinguished service record or that you had done so many great and magnificent deeds on the frontiers."

Doyle grinned. He made no reply. He knew that Petra was speaking for the benefit of the scanners watching them, spying on them. Although he had many questions to ask her, he did not dare voice them, even couched in mnemonic language. She seemed to read his thoughts. She smiled encouragingly. "Doyle, the first chance we get, I should like to spend a few hours in contemplation in the Gardens of Mnemosyne. Would you like to join me?"

"Now that's the best idea I've heard in days," he said as the door opened and they stepped into the corridor leading to his quarters. "Yes, I would like very much to join you."

She glanced toward the surveillance monitors. Then she turned and smiled at him. "Now that," she said with a laugh, "is a most revolutionary thing for you to do."

He laughed and got the meaning of her hidden message.

7

Kinsmen

Doyle and Petra left the citadel for the first time unaccompanied by guards. They stepped onto the moving sidewalk, then to the express lane that led through a series of sleek tunnels straight to the sanctuary of the Gardens of Mnemosyne. Petra laughed aloud when she noticed him glancing around apprehensively. "Don't worry about being followed now that you've been inaugurated and are a national celebrity. They're not following us any more. Not only that, but we've the right of sanctuary without surveillance in the gardens."

A little puzzled, Doyle gave her a questioning glance.

Petra explained, keeping her voice low so as not to be overheard. "The ceremony officially established you as a national hero. That is why the Secretariat dismissed your guards. By now every citizen and servoman on the planet knows your face, and there is nowhere you could go without being recognized. Your name will soon become a household word. The Secretariat has seen to it that you are made a legend in your own time."

"You're putting me on?"

Petra laughed. In the artificial light of the tunnel through which they were being transported her features were highlighted in such a way that Doyle suddenly began to see her in a new way. Although he had remained somewhat aloof and inattentive to her because he had always taken her for granted, he was realizing now that she was a truly lovely woman. Beautiful, in fact. It occurred to him at that moment that he had been a fool. "No, my sweet," she said, "I'm not putting you on. You were placed incommunicado until the Secretariat had completed their program to install you as a figure of . . ."

"*Figurehead?*" he grinned. "Shouldn't that be the word?"

She averted her eyes. "Don't be bitter. That very well may be, so why fight it?" She searched his face and smiled.

Doyle shrugged. "They're setting me up to become a scapegoat."

"You catch on quick."

Doyle laughed. "I wish I could do something just as quick."

"You just might be able to do something—quick."

He nodded. "Are you suggesting that you have help to offer?"

"I might."

"Can we recruit others?" he asked.

"It will be difficult—but we can. The demonstrators at the public meeting are only too willing to help."

"But dare we risk contacting them? Surely, they're being watched closely, are they not?"

"Yes. But to do what needs to be done will require a great deal of risk—and we'll need to deal with people who may or may not be trustworthy."

"Thanks for the warning."

"Don't mention it." She laughed and pressed his hand in hers fondly. "If all goes well, darling," she said with a promise in her tone, "and we are not being watched when we go into the gardens, I just may have a pleasant surprise for you."

He peered at her.

Petra explained in a cautious whisper, "The underground coalition—the Chamberists—have asked to meet with you. I'm to bring you to them if all is clear and we're not followed."

"The *Chamberists?*" he said with a surprised smile.

"Yes. You *are* surprised to learn that we have not been sitting idly by while the Secretariat imposes its totalitarian shackles on us. I'm glad you're surprised."

"I'm pleased too."

Petra nudged him. They had arrived at the exit, and it was time to step across the moving beltway to the crossover that led into the gardens. Before they emerged and once again entered the surveillance area, Petra said in a guarded tone, "If all goes well and we are able to slip undetected beyond the detector net, I'll take you to the secret meeting place."

"Here in the gardens?"

She smiled. "Can you think of a better place? Right under their noses. Since they outlawed the public meeting places and the recreation cafés, there was no place for us to get together."

They crossed a second beltway and reached the foliage-lined walk leading into the Gardens of Mnemonsyne. From somewhere nearby the sound of tolling carillons was heard. In the distance the sound of space transports being launched was audible. An occasional passerby was met on the path and they barely exchanged glances as they passed, though one or two persons took second looks at Doyle and smiled to indicate they recognized him and wished him well. Just as they went through the gate, a group of students recognized Doyle and came running over, surrounding him, asking for his autograph. Several of the students stood at the fringes of the crowd, looking on, scowls on their faces. One young man made a menacing gesture as if to hurl something at Doyle. Before he could take aim a beam of light flashed down from one of the scanners, immobilizing him. The crowd turned and stared as two guards appeared out of nowhere and dragged him away. Petra and Doyle exchanged apprehensive glances.

Doyle signed the autographs and they moved on.

They turned down a secluded path that led to the statue of the mother of the muses, Mnemosyne. Doyle nodded incredulously. "It's been years, hasn't it, Petra? Everything seems changed, different somehow from the way I remember it here."

"Yes, everything has changed."

She paused and stopped him. They glanced around and quickly moved down a secluded path where the surveillance gear was less abundant. "Yes," she said again, "the new order made many changes, but of course," she said when they came into range of an obvious scanner on a lamp post at the edge of the path, "all the changes are for the better."

The cynicism in her tone was apparent. "But of course," he said for the benefit of their secret auditors.

Following the path leading away from the gigantic statue of Mnemosyne, they arrived at the rotunda, where the statues of the Nine Muses—the legendary daughters of the mother of memory, Mnemosyne—representing all the branches of knowledge, faced the nine garden paths leading in the various directions to the labyrinths. The gardens were intended primarily to be used by the citizenry for contemplation and self-instruction. However the paths were little used, overgrown with moss and shrubs.

As they descended into the labyrinth, which was now almost completely overgrown with neglected vines and foliage, Petra cautioned Doyle to be silent and to do as she did. He followed her movements, stopping when she did, as they made their way along the little-used path. Finally when they reached the statue of Euterpe, the goddess of music, they stopped. They moved beneath a thick growth of shrubbery and Petra activated the audio console set in stone beside the statue at the base. At once the area was immersed in the delightful strains of Grieg's *Holberg Suite.* It was one of Doyle's favorites from his university days. He stood for several minutes listening, reflecting, remembering the days of his youth. He smiled and pressed Petra's hand fondly. He drew a deep breath and said, "It's been a great while, hasn't it?"

"Seems like eons," she said. "It makes me think of those happy days," she said a little wistfully.

Doyle was choked with nostalgia as he looked down into her misted eyes. He had to look away from her. His memory was too keen, and for once he wished he could forget. He had regretted for many years his decision not to marry Petra and settle down. He had often wondered how his life would have been had he not elected to join the pioneer forces.

They began walking again, toward the pillars of justice, which had been erected to the memory of past orders of law years before the Justivac had been constructed and put into use. A keystone dedication plaque below it fixed the date as the third year of the colony, for all posterity to see. Doyle noted that new inscriptions had been placed on the smooth facets above it in a more prominent place. The legend stated simply that the new order of the Justivac had been installed and was the ultimate in the administration of justice for all. It was installed in the year of "Momentous Historic Occasions, 2091."

Nodding with dissatisfaction at the tablets in a kind of dismayed refusal to accept what was inscribed there, Doyle looked at Petra. He caught a glimpse of something meaningful in her eyes. "For nine years," she said quietly, "we have lived and thrived in peace and harmony with freedom and justice for all . . ." Her tone was hollow and her gaze now vacant.

Doyle did not smile. He knew Petra meant the opposite of what she had said. It was dialect—the propaganda that the Secretariat had been drumming into the populace. Her words had been for the benefit of their hidden auditors.

"Thanks to the Justivac," Doyle added, remembering something he had seen many times, "man has no need of judges or juries of his peers, lawyers, courts, or any of the decadent methods of doling out justice still practiced on earth. All the worthwhile laws legislated by the former advanced societies and civilizations of the decadent past and all the decisions of the great justices of old have been fed into the Justivac computer; it now dispenses justice without prejudice and no longer requires we the people to depend upon his inferior fellow man for due process. The Justivac takes care of that for us. It is better to live by the laws as interpreted by the computer than it is to be at the mercy of one's fellow man. We are now free of the imperfection of man, who is susceptible to prejudice, bias, false witness, and bribery."

Petra said woodenly, "Yes, it is better. With the Justivac, all things are equal and fair. All laws have been programmed into its memory as well as all the just decisions; we no longer need to depend on our inferior brothers to mete out our justice. Justice is now swift and expedient. The Justivac is the ultimate in perfection."

They exchanged several distressed glances. Now they knew their auditors would relax their vigilant surveillance, and they might be able to move about more freely without being watched so closely—they hoped.

It pained Doyle to say things he did not believe, but they were both at the mercy of their auditors. He knew without ever having asked Petra that this sort of conversation was necessary if they were to remain above suspicion.

"Dear," Petra said finally, taking him by the hand, "let's govern ourselves from now on so we'll be paragons of virtue—models after which the citizens can pattern themselves. This is the golden opportunity as the bourgeiosie used to say, to rise above them and prove ourselves worthy of membership in the legion that follows the Secretariat. Since the Secretariat has seen fit to make you a famous man anyway, don't you agree it would be wise for us to set ourselves out as perfect loyal citizens?"

Her words were false to Doyle, and he wondered if their secret auditors had also detected the note of artificiality in what she had said. He believed she knew what she was doing.

He realized that the Secretariat had recruited hundreds of citizens years before the new order had been made the law of the land and these citizens who were not posted in the listening posts were for the most part dullards and ne'er-do-wells too lazy to work and quite satisfied to spend their duty hours spying on their fellows. All incentive for promotion and initiative for attaining worthwhile goals had been discouraged for the people in this corps and mediocrity was the rule. With this in mind, he knew Petra knew exactly what she was doing when she had given voice to the party line mottoes.

"Yes," he said finally, without enthusiasm, "that's a good idea. Now that I've been invested with this chance to serve the Secretariat, I feel you're right. I ought to do something to distinguish myself and prove to our citizens that I am worthy of the office."

"Oh, darling," Petra beamed, touching his arm, "you *are* worthy. Look there—the waterfall of Mnemosyne! Shall we take off our shoes and wade beneath it like we used to do when we were at the university together?"

"Yes, yes," he laughed, running beside her now, his hand in hers. "It'll be like old times." Suddenly he knew. Suddenly he realized that once they went into the shallow water and waded beneath the miniature falls, which they called "Little Niagara," they would soon be out of range of the audiovisual scanners.

They arrived at the edge of the pool at the foot of the falls and removed their footwear. Hand-in-hand, they stepped into the cool water and waded toward the cascade that tumbled down from huge overhanging cliffs. The roar was deafening, and the fine spray against their cheeks was as refreshing as being in a rain forest. A rain forest of sweet nature unpolluted by humans and electronic eyes that spied. As soon as they were beneath the cascade, Petra's hand tightened in his. "Hurry," she had to shout to be heard, "we're late for the rendezvous."

"Where're we going?" Doyle asked, peering about them. He could see nothing except the rocks and sheer face of the cliff beneath the cascade.

"You shall see. Between these boulders. We approach and wait a moment for the hidden sentries to recognize us. Once they see us, they will activate a photon screen on which our images will be projected. That way the Secretariat's spies will be able to watch us, though we'll be well out of audio range. They'll believe we're just cavorting—and making love."

They reached a rock and climbed across it. A moment later there was a mistlike screen behind them. Doyle watched in fascination as their images were projected on it. They seemed tridimensional and quite alive. From the banks of the pool he knew it would look as if they were acting just as normally as before, and it would be impossible to detect that the figures that represented them were little more than illusion.

They climbed down the edge of the rock and slid into the pool on the other side, wading in knee-deep water toward what Doyle swore looked like solid rock. When they were within three feet of the granite surface, the rock tilted to the right, and two men armed with cyclonder pistols motioned them inside. They stepped over the vault threshold, and the boulder closed behind him. Petra smiled at Doyle, pride and amusement in her eyes. "What do you think of our secret underground complex?"

He looked around in amazement at the highly sophisticated network of corridors containing everything from food processing and storage units to electronic surveillance gear and banks of computers. "Ingenious!" he muttered. In a large chamber to his right he saw men and women sitting at benches constructing microelectronic devices. When he had looked around several times, still astonished, he asked, "How is this possible right in the heart of Mnemosyne? Who is in this with you? How long has this been going on?"

Petra pressed her fingertips to his lips. "Darling, one

question at a time. Come with me now. The council is meeting and everyone's waiting to meet you."

He looked at her and in the artificial light her eyes glinted happily, hopefully. Then she took him by the hand and they walked barefoot toward a corridor beside which two guards stood. The guards smiled and stepped aside to let them pass. They descended a sloping ramp to a lower level and entered an arched door that opened onto a huge cavernlike chamber. Inside, seated at a massive table upon which was a model of the City of Mnemosyne, were twelve men and women. Doyle recognized some of them. Distinguished physicists, biochemists, astrogeologists, and scientists—people he knew and respected. Then he recalled something that made him halt dead in his tracks. The scientists were all alleged to be *dead!* Was he looking at a council of dead people? Then he recalled that the Secretariat had announced the "deaths" of the individuals who were now seated before him. One by one they had mysteriously vanished—and now they were all here. How was such a thing possible?

"You are staring, Commandant Doyle," said a distinguished, gray-haired man at the head of the table. "Come and be seated," he said, waving Doyle and Petra to vacant places at the opposite end of the long table. "Your questions will be duly answered."

Doyle went to the table and held out the chair for Petra. She seated herself. Then he stood behind the second vacant chair and leaned upon it. He looked at each man and woman in turn, nodding in disbelief.

"Forgive me for staring," he said finally, "but I was of the impression that all of you were dead."

"But of course," replied the spokesman at the far end of the table. "We had to die in order to leave Mnemosyne and dedicate our lives to overthrowing the Secretariat and their infernal Justivac machine. It was the only way."

Doyle looked around. He nodded and said, "I know you. I

83

know all of you. We were on the first transport together." He blinked and pointed at the gray-haired man. "You are Dr. Tayon, number twelve." He turned and stared at the woman at the doctor's side. "You are Dr. Nunn. Number twenty-three. You and Dr. Tayon are medical doctors." He paused again and began to call every name.

"Dr. Mann, number thirty-two. Astrobiologist."

He waited for the nod and went to the next individual.

"Dr. Royce, number forty. You developed the Royce system for hand-computer diagnosis and treatment."

"I did. And for that the Secretariat wanted to reward me. They tried to make a servoman of me. They said I was too dangerous because of my beliefs."

"Yes, I remember," Doyle said. "You were against the movement from the start. You were the only one who dared speak out against them."

All heads nodded.

Doyle turned toward a young man with a high forehead and a thin scar across his left cheek. "You, sir, are the famous Dr. Louis who developed the Louis system of holography."

"You and I shared the same stateroom on the transport the first week out."

"Yes, we never did get to finish that chess game, did we?"

"And you madam," Doyle smiled at a silver-haired woman, "are Dr. Chinn, the prize-winning physicist. The entire scientific fraternity was up in arms back on earth when they heard you had volunteered for the expedition."

"That was a long time ago, wasn't it?" she said. "Seventeen years by our reckoning of time—eons by Petra's time and by the time of those born here after the warp. We are the old ones. It was better for us to disappear than to stay and be throttled by the Secretariat regime."

Doyle leaned forward still further over his chair. He peered at a wizened old man seated beside her. "Dr. Joyko, Number sixty-seven. Medical doctor, surgeon, director of the organ bank, developer of the synthetic—"

"Ancient history!" interrupted Dr. Joyko with a touch of bitterness. "I was one of the first to defect. I joined with Dr. Tayon and Dr. Mann when construction was first begun on this secret underground complex. We were the ones who saw it all coming. But what could we do when we had no voices—when we were locked away in our clinics and hospitals and research centers, guarded by those totalitarian knaves?"

"Thank God you did what you did," Doyle said. "Now at least we have a chance. I was beginning to give up hope when I returned and saw all that had happened here."

"Yes, we all joined together," Dr. Tayon explained, "when we saw there was no other way and that there would be a long, long wait before the others would come around to seeing the handwriting in the sand. We carefully arranged for our 'deaths' and came here to live."

"It was very clever of you to locate here right under the city," Doyle said. He recalled the names of the others at the table one by one and then after he had correctly identified the last man as Dr. Boyer, number ninety-four, nuclear physicist, developer of the ion core power system, he seated himself beside Petra.

"Now that you are here and we have made this good beginning," Dr. Tayon addressed Doyle, "it is my duty as the twelfth member of the original expedition and as the senior presiding Chamberist to ask you, on behalf of all of us here, will you take part in our revolution?"

Doyle looked around at them and slowly rose. He said in a firm tone, "I will take part in your revolution—*gladly*. I am opposed to the new order, the Secretariat, the Justivac, *and* most important of all, I am against the future development and use of the mind-erasing Orrery device. I trust you are in accord?" He paused and looked around again. Every head nodded affirmatively.

Dr. Tayon motioned Doyle to be seated. He put his hands together and then through narrowed eyes studied Doyle from across the table for a long, searching moment. When he finally spoke, his voice was grim and wooden. "Commandant Doyle, we have searched for six years for the right man to lead our rebellion."

"And?"

"You're the man we need."

Doyle blinked and leaned back. He was shocked. "But why *me?*"

"Because you are the only one still in power who can help us."

"What do you mean, *still* in power?"

Dr. Tayon smiled knowingly. "You don't suppose for a moment that you're going to be allowed to remain in charge of that complex for very long, do you? The Secretariat has other plans for you. First, they will subvert your mind—perhaps even convert you into a servoman."

Doyle took it calmly. He believed that. Anything was possible on the planet now that the Secretariat had risen to power, and he knew they would not hesitate to enslave him if it suited their diabolical purposes.

"There will be a rebellion," Dr. Tayon said. "I fear that force may be necessary to overthrow them—but I hope it doesn't come to that. I hope that you, being free for the moment, will find a way to overthrow them without bloodshed."

"Have you a plan?" Doyle asked.

"Quite frankly, we have several plans—but none of them are feasible. We can implement any plan, and we have many alternatives. That's why we've labored for so long building this underground complex. And why we've been waiting patiently for a man like you—a young man with initiative and stamina who can lead, administrate, and gain entry into the Orrery and the other citadels without arousing suspicion." He paused and cleared his throat. He glanced around at the others and received hopeful glances and encouraging nods. All eyes turned toward Doyle again as Dr. Tayon continued. "We know of your convictions and have followed your career for many years. Your latest exploit is also known to us, and we almost regret that you stopped the alien invaders. Rule under them might have been more tolerable than what we have now. But that's beside the point. Thanks to Petra and the efforts of the other Chamberists who have infiltrated the new order and the Secretariat at all levels except your own, we are now ready. It took us three years to secretly program the Justivac so it would recommend you for the position at the Orrery. When Petra's grandfather allegedly died, his demise had been timed precisely so your name would be nominated by the machine—after Petra and a few of her trusted confederates had programmed it to nominate you."

Doyle glanced toward Petra, then looked at Dr. Tayon. "Are you saying Commandant Boden is *not* dead?"

All heads nodded. Dr. Tayon replied, "No, thank God. He is still very much alive. At the present he is in the laboratory working with our staff in an effort to develop a system that would neutralize the cyclonder system—and the Orrery device. But, alas, so far we've been unsuccessful. Although we believe we've solved the equations and are currently constructing some prototypes, we have no device capable of face-to-face confrontation with the weapons of the Secretariat. The people have been disarmed completely and are wholly at the mercy of them."

Doyle's face brightened. He smiled. This was the first ray of hope he had had since being placed in the command.

"When Commandant Boden managed to get word to us that the Secretariat was planning to subvert the Orrery for their own diabolical purposes against the people—to enslave every man, woman, and child on the planet—we at first thought he was mad. But when our intelligence confirmed his report, it was too late to do anything. Fortunately for us you were elevated to hero status, and we took the opportunity to engineer your appointment."

"But again I ask, why me?" Doyle inquired.

"Because," Dr. Tayon replied, "we need a man of youth, one who can act, and one who knows how to think for himself. Out there you will be on your own. You are the only one for this mission. You have proved yourself as a brave and courageous man, a leader of men, and a man unafraid of speaking his own mind. Now that you know our secrets, and some of the secrets of the Orrery, and have been programmed by the Justivac and have been lionized as a hero of the colony, you are our logical choice, and—I might also add—our only hope."

"But wouldn't Commandant Boden have been a better choice?" Doyle said. "I located his sanctum, and I have seen his atomic clock self-destruct device. Only a most ingenious and astute man such as he could have accomplished all that right under the spying eyes of the Secretariat."

Dr. Tayon smiled. He nodded. "As I said before, we need a man of your youth. To accomplish what Dr. Boden set out to do will require much fortitude and physical strength. I'm not quite certain that I understand fully what remains to be done—however Boden planned it, but he cannot carry it off. He is up in years and physically unfit for such a herculean chore. What you accomplished on that desolate plain against the invaders proves you are capable of the job that must be done."

"What about the atomic clock?" Doyle asked. "I'm not quite sure I understand its function."

"It is a doomsday device. It is set to completely destroy the Orrery citadel. We have not yet decided to do that—if there's another way."

Doyle nodded and, after several minutes of deep thought, said, "My first officer, Kagan. He presents a problem. He's not let me go near the complex and only allowed me to leave my quarters in the company of armed aides—until I was inaugurated. I believe he's a spy—that he's been made my aide solely to watch me."

"You believe correctly," said Dr. Joyko. He rose and riffled through several envelopes on the conference table, which stood next to the model of the citadel. He withdrew two film cubes and dropped them into the viewing cup. At once the image came into focus in the tridimensional form. Those present could see Kagan entering the hall of the Justivac. The image grew fuzzy, and the figures went out of focus for several moments. The doctor hastened to explain, "We had the hall monitored, and after several months we confirmed that Kagan is a Secretariat henchman."

Then Kagan's image was seen and his voice heard with great clarity. "I cannot be certain of her loyalty, though I believe she is in love with me and therefore will betray Doyle should it develop that he is in league with those in the conspiracy against the Secretariat."

Petra's gaze was turned upward toward Doyle when he glanced at her for confirmation. She smiled and said in a low voice, "Now you know the truth. I've been working undercover for three years, the last two pretending to be in love with Kagan."

The flicker of anguish in her eyes was concealed when she lowered her head and averted her gaze. She had seen something in Doyle's eyes too—and it pained her to know she had hurt him.

Doyle remained silent. His attention was riveted on the viewer. He watched as Kagan stood on the concordance keystone. He marveled at the ingenuity of the Chamberists in getting the surveillance device into such a hallowed, well-guarded place. It gave him confidence to think they had such well-placed spies within the enemy stronghold.

After several moments Doyle frowned at the silence that was now accompanying the image, and he asked Dr. Joyko,

"Why didn't the hidden viewer record the programming Kagan received?"

"When one is on the keystone, the audio is fed to the auditor via laser ribbon and cannot be tapped or monitored since it is beamed directly into the programmee's skull."

"And the Secretariat?" Doyle asked as the film came to an abrupt conclusion. "Who are those responsible? How many are involved? Where do they meet? What are their goals? And what else should I know about them?" He paused and looked around at the faces of the individuals seated at the table.

Dr. Tayon glanced at the others and spoke for them. "The Secretariat very cleverly meets in the sphere above the Justivac hall. No one knows who they are, when they meet, or for that matter, anything else about them. As you know, when the new order was established and the Justivac became the arm of justice here on 143, our elections were held as before—but with one novel twist. No one anywhere on the planet knows who was elected to office. All runners-up as well as those elected are kept incognito in the various citadels."

"Then the elections could have been phony too?" Doyle said.

"There's no doubt about it. Since anyone who dared to run for office was neither seen nor heard from again, who is to know what happened?" Dr. Tayon paused and rubbed his eyes. He spoke again, trying to keep his voice low and controlled. It was obvious that he was upset and on the threshold of losing control of his emotions. "For all we know, there may *not* be a Secretariat of twenty-six duly elected representatives; but instead we may be under the power of one or more arch-criminals."

Dr. Joyko looked at Doyle. "You seem disturbed by this," he observed.

Doyle nodded. "I am." He paused and looked around at them. "I appreciate your confidence in me—but are you certain I'm your man?"

Dr. Tayon rose. He motioned several of the others to remain silent when they started to speak out. He looked at Doyle and said, "We're certain of nothing. All we can say is that you're our only hope—our *last* hope. If you fail, it may be years, maybe decades, before we'll have another opportunity to overthrow the tyrants. First, you must find a way to neutralize the Orrery. Second, you must make the Justivac inoperative. Third, you must find a way to remove from power those who have usurped the rightful authority our constitution guaranteed all citizens. This will pave the way toward freedom with open elections again."

"And fourth," spoke out Dr. Nunn with blazing eyes, "we must insure that such a thing will never happen again. Once we are able to immobilize the forces of the Secretariat, we will succeed. You *must* find a way to accomplish this, Commandant Doyle. Then all we seek may come to pass."

"That's a tall order," Doyle said. "I doubt if I can do it."

"No! No!" a dozen voices cried out. "You *can* find a way to do these things—you must! If we're to survive, you must find a way."

"Yes, Commandant Doyle," said Dr. Tayon. "You must succeed. Even though we command a wealth of equipment, resources, and supplies that we've managed to smuggle in here during the past years, we cannot move against the Secretariat openly until the time is ripe. It must be done from within, not from without. Like the Communists did when they took over the United States and all the other countries of the Western Hemisphere on earth in the last years of the twentieth century. Let's take a cue from them and do what they did. All that we've stockpiled here will be at your disposal, and you may have complete command of all our operations. Your wish is our command."

"I see," Doyle mused. "But I just don't know. I'm only one man . . ."

Petra rose. She touched his arm. Her fingers rested on his

91

sleeve and lightly caressed his flesh beneath the cloth. When the others fell silent she spoke. "Doyle, we've discussed this for months. We've voted on it, and the decision has been made. You are our only hope. Our last hope in our lifetime!"

Doyle drew a deep breath and exhaled. He gazed around at their intent faces and knew at that moment that he could not disappoint them. He felt humble and awed at the power they had placed in his hands, and he dared not to let thoughts of self-doubt creep into his mind. "Very well," he said with a sigh of finality. "Where do I begin?"

Everyone sighed in relief. Smiles of contentment and hope appeared on every face. Finally, Dr. Tayon spoke. "There is only one place to begin—that is here in our underground headquarters. We will familiarize you with our ordnance and equipment and of course with our staff and personnel. Most important you will command our fighting forces and our espionage-sabotage network. You will coordinate all operations. You shall have carte blanche to draw men and equipment from our stockpiles. You are now our commander in chief and may God go with you. We are yours to command." Dr. Tayon bowed his head and offered a prayer. All heads bowed.

Doyle smiled when the benediction was over. He rose and leaned on the table with clenched fists. He gazed around at every face and after a long, thoughtful moment, said, "I am deeply honored by your trust in me. All I can say is that I shall try my best to succeed—or die in the attempt."

Everyone rose, applauding. The women cried openly. The men looked at him with wan smiles on their lips. Dr. Tayon walked around the table and clapped a hand on Doyle's shoulder.

8

Custodial

A moment after Doyle and Petra left the underground complex, they paused to have one final word in privacy beneath the screen of the rushing waters of the falls, free for one final moment from prying eyes, free from the scanners that they knew were frantically searching for them.

"Darling," she said, halting him when he drew away from her and avoided her caresses, "please wait. I know how you must feel learning about Kagan and myself in such a way. I know it must've been a shock for you to learn I've been his—"

"I understand," he said flatly. "Say no more about it. It's been a long time. I've never expected you to carry the torch—"

"You're cruel. I'm trying to convey something to you, and you won't listen."

He looked at her and nodded. "This isn't the time or place for that. They're searching for us."

She paled and clutched his arm, peering out beneath the waterfall. A squad of guards armed with cyclonders was seen moving slowly along the pool's edge beyond. They were about to begin wading into the pool toward the falls.

"There isn't a moment to lose!" she cried, suddenly pulling him into the water beside her. "Hold me and let's float out under the falls. Something happened to the camouflage. They can't see our pictures. We'll pretend we were making love and wanted privacy."

"It'll only make more trouble," Doyle said. "Kagan will never forgive you if you've made him fall in love with you."

"I'd rather risk that than lead them to the kinsmen underground."

"I wouldn't worry about that. The shields I noticed inside the granite entrance cannot be penetrated by probing devices or detectors."

"Still," she said, desperately pulling him into the knee-deep water, "why take the risk?"

Doyle slid into the shallow water and embraced her. They floated on the surface and drifted out beneath the cascade and emerged in the deep pool on the other side within view of the patrol.

The thundering waterfall drowned out all sound. They knew the guardsmen were shouting to them, but they pretended not to hear or see them. Not until they were in the center of the pool, laughing and hugging each other, acting like cavorting children, did they pause finally and look toward the pool's edge where the guardsmen had assembled. The corporal in charge angrily beckoned to them and shouted, "Come ashore at once. We have orders to escort you to the Orrery complex to First Officer Kagan."

Doyle and Petra paddled to the shallow end and then waded ashore. The guardsmen helped them over the granite footing and then formed ranks with them at the center. They marched in step rapidly toward the labyrinth and then left the gardens through the emergency turnstile that ascended to the express conveyor transport. As they sped along through the network of tunnels and then entered the lifts that carried them up above the weathersphere to the complex, neither Petra nor Doyle uttered a word. They were fully aware of the watchful eyes observing them through the scanners, and they knew their every word and gesture was being recorded to be later scrutinized and analyzed by behaviorists and their cology meters. Instinctively they knew they ought to behave as though guilty of misconduct in a public place, and they did so. To behave in a nonchalant fashion would be tantamount to an admission of dishonesty; to behave in a surreptitious manner would be to betray themselves as co-conspirators.

Their clothing was dry by the time they arrived at the guard station on the Orrery security level. The escort halted at the door to the interrogation room and stepped aside to permit them to pass. Doyle went after Petra, stooping in order to pass beneath a low-mounted sensor that inspected them for possible weapons and contraband. The precaution of the sensing equipment was standard. Since the new order of the Secretariat had begun, such security measures were common-place in governmental departments in which secret documents and classified equipment were located.

Doyle had a disgruntled expression on his face. He was impatient with all that had happened and annoyed at being subjected to arrest and sensor search. He decided to give vent to his feelings and use this as a test of his true station. He was anxious to learn whether or not he held the commandant's post merely as a powerless, titular figurehead or if he was really invested with authority commensurate with his rank and the command he was charged to administer.

Kagan entered, flanked by two uniformed aides.

"See here, Kagan!" blustered Doyle, stepping forward. "I resent your effrontery. Since when does a first officer overstep his rank and arrest his commanding officer? And I'd also like to know why I'm under surveillance."

"I am in command of this complex," Kagan said flatly. "The Secretariat charged me with the duty of seeing to your welfare and safety since you are such an important man now that you've been honored with the post of Orrery Commandant."

"I don't give a sine wave if you're in charge of the chamber pots!" cried Doyle. "I demand an explanation!"

Kagan's face darkened in anger. His eyes narrowed and his

95

brooding forehead was furrowed in frowns. He had to clench his fists in order to contain his anger. Then he smiled and said, "Please accept my deepest apologies, Commandant Doyle, sir. As your aide it is my duty to protect you from assassins."

"Assassins? You're joking."

"Quite the contrary, sir. High-ranking officials are often the target of conspirators these days."

"Since when?" demanded Doyle.

"For some time now. There's a conspiracy afoot, or didn't you know?"

"I know nothing of any such thing. I've been virtually a prisoner since my return from the frontier. How could I possibly know? And besides, I don't believe it. The city is under total surveillance by the monitoring devices, which seem to be concealed everywhere." Doyle gave Petra a warning glance. Then he turned and shouted at Kagan, "You're lying! I demand that you release us at once."

The two guardsmen elevated their cyclonders. Doyle noticed this and stared fiercely at them. Kagan, aware of the exchange and of Doyle's apparent loss of patience, motioned for the men to lower their weapons and go. As they went through the automatic door, Kagan's expression mellowed. He smiled feebly and, without glancing toward Petra, said, "What were you two doing, and how was it that you managed to elude the range of the scanners?"

"I don't know," Doyle said, then added, "and furthermore, I don't think it's any of your business what we were doing."

Kagan became grim again. He glared at them and said, "I may be the first officer here and you may outrank me, Doyle, but I am still in charge of security, and on this matter you are commanded to answer to me unless you prefer that I audit you in the presence of the Secretariat in the Justivac court."

"Is that threat supposed to frighten me?" Doyle said. "I don't give a damn one way or the other. I am in command here, and I won't tolerate this sort of thing from one of my

96

subordinates. In fact, I just might have *you* court-martialed for this. You're out of bounds, mister!"

Petra stepped forward. "Please both of you, stop this! Surely we can settle this amicably."

"Stay out of this, Petra," Kagan said, his gaze angry, his eyes fixed intently on Doyle. "I'm certain you had nothing to do with whatever happened."

"That's where you're wrong," Petra said. "We went into the pool and made love."

Kagan, stiffening slightly, turned and stared at her. He backed off a step and then narrowed his eyes. "Is that the truth?"

"Yes. I wanted to be with Doyle for old time's sake. We took off our shoes and went for a dip. Then we went around the waterfall where we could be alone. I didn't know we were being watched, and I didn't know you lost visual and audio contact with us when we went under the waterfall."

Kagan's expression had become an unmasked frown of hostility. He glared contemptuously at Petra, then he said to Doyle, "All right, I'll accept your excuse this time. But let me go on record as saying that I will not tolerate such things again."

"What's that supposed to mean," asked Doyle, "that we're not allowed to go off by ourselves again? That you must give us permission if we want to be together—*alone?*"

Kagan was furious, but he managed to contain his emotions. He said through narrowed lips, his voice a vehement hiss, "I told you I am in charge of the security in this complex—and I am also responsibility for your protection. I will not tolerate you being out of sight of the scanners."

"May we leave now?" Doyle said.

"By all means," Kagan replied, defeated. "You're free to go."

Petra turned toward the exit. Doyle paused a moment and said to Kagan, "I will change clothes and then meet you here. I want you to take me on a tour of the facilities and acquaint me with my duties. I've been patient long enough and will not tolerate being inactive any longer."

Kagan averted his gaze and, turning toward the opposite door, said, "Very well. I'll meet you here in an hour."

"And Petra accompanies me."

"No, that's not permitted. Only the commandant and the first officer are permitted inside the Orrery complex. You will bring your unicard so I may validate it and have your voice prints programmed to open the security doors."

Doyle brusquely turned and followed Petra out into the corridor. Two aides accompanied them down to the transport tubes. As they stepped into the cab, one of the men respectfully snapped to attention and said, "With your permission, Aide Petra, your personal effects have been removed to a new apartment next to the commandant's quarters."

Petra smiled and nodded. The cab door closed, and they were whisked down to their quarters. "How nice," Petra smiled up at Doyle.

"What's that?"

"He called me Aide Petra. So I'm now number one." She laughed a girlish kind of laugh and pressed Doyle's hand against her cheek.

"Don't let it go to your head," Doyle said. Then he added tersely, "There's much to be done."

They stepped into the corridor and were met by two servomen who escorted them to their quarters. Outside the door to his quarters, Doyle paused and told her, "I'll be along to inspect your apartment as soon as I shave and change. Then I have some orders to give you. Might as well put you to work now since there's so much to be done."

Petra nodded and followed the servoman down to the doorway at the end of the corridor. The door opened, and she paused to glance back at Doyle before entering.

Fifteen minutes later Doyle had entered Petra's new apartment and was standing, aperitif in his hand, watching her as she explored the rooms. "I like it," she said, taking her cocktail from the tray that the servomaid had brought. "Do you know why I like it?"

Doyle shrugged. He continued to watch her, amusement in his eyes. Somehow she was unchanged. She was still the girl he had known many years ago.

"I grew up in these quarters," she said. "My piano was over there and my toy chest, there."

He watched as she pointed and moved about the living room. She stopped and looked into the bed chamber again and said, wistfully, "How very, very long ago that seems. I do wonder what happened to my toys and the things I used to have when I lived here with grandpapa."

"They were probably donated to the children's school," Doyle said.

"Yes," she nodded, lost in thought for a moment. "That's where they were sent—to the children who were born on the space transport."

At that moment the door opened, and they turned to see who had entered. One of the servomaids stood just inside the doorway, her expressionless face turned toward Doyle. "Commandant," she said in her almost mechanical monotone, "First Officer Kagan is awaiting you in the security chamber for dinner. Please accompany me, sir."

Doyle moved toward Petra and gave her a light kiss on the forehead. She said nothing and stood woodenly, watching him go. Her eyes were raptly fixed on him, and her face seemed aglow.

In the security chamber after he had inserted his unicard in the slot and recorded his voice print on it by stating his name and rank, Doyle found Kagan standing in front of a viewer.

He came forward and Kagan snapped to attention.

"At ease, Kagan," Doyle said. "If you don't mind, I'd

prefer it if you'd dispense with the formalities. Militarism offends me."

"If that is your wish."

"It is. Now what's on our agenda?"

"We'll have a simple dinner, and then I'll conduct you through the Orrery complex and familiarize you with your duties."

"And introduce me to the staff?"

"There is no staff."

"You must be joking?"

"No, sir. Everything has been automatized, and only a skeleton crew of technicians is maintained in this complex. The duties of commandant and first officer are to personally maintain, test, and operate the units."

"Without assistance?"

"That is correct."

"And what of all the guards I've seen milling about this citadel?"

"They weren't milling about. They're on patrol."

"You must have an entire division posted here."

"No, not that many. Just two hundred security guards. The noncoms are regular guards. The rest are servos."

"Servomen as armed guards?" exclaimed Doyle. "Since *when* is that being done? I clearly recall that a law was passed forbidding the use of servopeople in military service or as security guards. Moreover, it was absolutely forbidden to program them to bear arms."

"The Secretariat saw fit to change that ridiculous law."

"They saw fit to subvert it, you mean!"

Kagan's face darkened. His eyes narrowed, and he said, "That is a seditious statement. I'd guard my tongue if I were you, Commandant, sir."

Doyle said nothing further. He went to the table and sat down. Kagan joined him and pressed the buzzer at his right on the chair arm. A servomaid entered, carrying a tray.

"Drink?" Kagan asked, helping himself to one of the two aperitif glasses on the tray.

"No. But don't let me stop you."

"I didn't intend that you should," he said curtly, sipping his drink and watching Doyle's reaction.

Doyle stared at him fixedly, determined not to waver under his gaze. He was measuring Kagan, trying to decide in his own mind what sort of a man he really was, and what he was after. He decided to prod him. "Why do you resent me, Kagan?"

The question caught him unawares. He lowered his drink and forced a smile. "I resent you because you're not one of us. You represent the decadent past. Though we are the same age, you are still existing in another time era—an era that still foolishly clings to altruistic ideas."

"And you belong to the new era—the Secretariat's new order?"

"Yes, most definitely. I am dedicated to that cause. I cannot see their logic or the logic of the Justivac in recommending one such as you for the post that by all rights should have gone to me."

"You are envious."

"True. But only because you are in command here and I should be in command instead."

"At least you are direct and honest—a most admirable quality," Doyle said. "But tell me, Kagan, is your resentment going to affect the operations here?"

"Certainly not. I am a dedicated man, first and foremost. Nothing shall stand in the way of my doing my duty. I've sworn to uphold the standards no matter what differences or obstacles may threaten to stand in my way. If necessary, I would be forced to kill you if you did anything to impede me in my duties or if you did anything that might endanger the Orrery complex."

"Yet, I am your commanding officer and your rival."

A bit nettled, Kagan squinted at Doyle. "Rival?"

"Yes," Doyle said with a touch of irony, "I've taken Petra away from you, and that has damaged your ego. I've been placed in command of the Orrery, and that has crushed you."

"It has *not* crushed me. Lest you forget, I am a *Secretariatist*, and that authority is higher than that of a commandant."

"Who can forget in *this* land where all men are sworn to live by the mind code?" Doyle laughed thinly. A second servomaid entered, carrying a tray laden with covered dishes that she began to set on the table before them. "Once, many decades ago, on earth, there was a man called Hitler. He had his Secretariatists too. Only they were called the Gestapo."

"Hitler?" said Kagan, frowning. "Who was he?"

9

Trial

Doyle was impressed by the simplicity of the Orrery complex. The consoles were operable by one man from the central command post, which overlooked the gigantic dynamotors and the impulsators.

Above the domed observatory was a replica of the celestial bodies in their exact coordinates. Window dressing, Doyle thought to himself. He saw that the slightest touch of a toggle switch could activate the ion field that in turn could broadcast alpha waves throughout the planet, at once immobilizing every human being who did not wear protective gear. Since the Secretariat had made it a capital offense for any citizens to own protective helmets of any type, and since all materials necessary to construct such shielded helmets were unavailable to the populace, Doyle knew they were at the Secretariat's mercy. Now he understood why so many former leading citizens had joined the Chamberist movement. It was their only hope. As he looked over the vast equipment, he realized that the programming he had received in the hall of the Justivac had been incomplete.

He walked beside Kagan as they went into the complex,

going down level after level, then up level after level. They paused during the inspection tour to gaze down into the seemingly bottomless gulf between the ion chambers and relays. It was an awesome sight. He knew that the Secretariat had had no intention of entrusting all the operations to him. They had too much at stake. He looked at Kagan with a new respect. Kagan was more than he pretended to be, and Doyle did not like it.

Now that he knew the awesome power over which he had *purportedly* been placed in command, he wondered if he could do anything to fight the Secretariat and the Justivac. Once the controls were activated, the Secretariat would within a few minutes have total command over every citizen. Their brain waves would be picked up by the machine's readout master, and they would be little more than robots, less than the servos, mindless beings serving only the will of the Secretariat. At the push of a button or the turning of a dial the entire population would be turned into slaves.

Doyle looked at Kagan as they peered into the black abyss between the ion chambers and wondered if they actually had entrusted him with such power. He decided not. He also decided that Kagan was *not* one of the Secretariat's inner circle. He was a lackey. Somewhere, he was certain, there existed a second console—a master. In all probability it was hidden in the locked chambers of the Secretariat. Moreover, Doyle reasoned, Kagan could *not* activate the Orrery unless he had been first ordered to do so by the Secretariat. Doyle knew that it would be futile for him to try to operate the controls for in all probability they were not operable unless the master switches were thrown first.

The operation of the ion belt was simple enough to understand. After programming the degree of power to be broadcast over the face of the planet, then setting the power level generators and governors, all that needed to be done was to press the switch. Doyle now knew that he could not do it, for the actual switch was located somewhere else and not in the Orrery.

From what he had seen of the security measures taken by Kagan in the complex, he understood why the kinsmen he had met in the underground headquarters were counting so heavily on him. Since no one else had been able to gain admission to the complex, it would be up to him to devise and then carry out a plan to immobilize the complex. But how?

When Doyle asked Kagan if the console was linked in tandem to a second master console somewhere else, Kagan squared his shoulders and glared at him indignantly. "What do *you* think, Commandant Doyle?"

"I think you're just a flunky. That you are, like me, simply a figurehead without authority—without power to do anything."

"For your enlightenment, Doyle—there is one thing I *do* have: the power of life and death—over *you*." Kagan's eyes narrowed, and his mouth closed with a snap of finality.

Doyle made no reply. He opened a cabinet to the right of the console and looked inside. To his surprise he found a complete tool shop conveniently at hand.

"We do our own maintenance here on the bridge," Kagan said. "No one else is permitted access."

Doyle feigned indifference to what Kagan had just said. "Security measure, no doubt."

"No doubt."

"And the schematics? Where are they?"

Kagan tapped his head and smiled. "As Secretariatist they are filed away up here."

"What if something should happen to you?" Doyle asked flatly. "Is such a drastic security measure wise?"

"The Justivac has it filed in its memory banks."

"And what if there is an emergency? What if the ion band goes awry during a routine measurement? What if a component breaks down and you are dead?"

Kagan laughed. "It can't happen. There is a failsafe mechanism built in."

"Yeah? Tell me more."

Kagan frowned. He eyed Doyle with suspicion. Then he drew a deep breath and with measured reluctance said, "The Secretariat has a committee that oversees operations at all times."

This is what Doyle had wanted to find out. He had not expected Kagan to be stupid enough to tell him this, and his hopes soared for the moment because he now knew where he stood. No doubt the consoles and every inch of the bridge were covered by audiovisual scanners and not a move could be made without being observed and duly recorded. How then could he accomplish what he needed to do?

"Something disturbs me, Kagan," he said after a moment of deliberation. "What kind of failsafe mechanism is there that would prevent accidental or deliberate triggering?"

Kagan laughed. "The Justivac's circuits are linked to it."

"But that makes it even more dangerous."

"Quite the contrary. The relays operate at lightning speed. Nothing can be done until the Justivac has ordered it done. If any attempt is made to subvert the trajectory or programming, the Justivac will neutralize the entire complex."

"And what if by some quirk the Justivac goes haywire? Machines have been known to break down, need I remind you?"

"No, you needn't remind me. But the Justivac *can't* break down. It's the ultimate in perfection. It even has the capability of repairing itself should one of the circuits fail. It reasons and it—"

"Is godlike?" interrupted Doyle.

Kagan nodded. "Yes, that would be a good analogy. The Justivac is something of a god."

Doyle scratched his head and yawned. "I think I've had it for today." He walked to the observation window and stared absently down at the dynamotors below. Without looking around at Kagan, he said with calculating deliberation, "I think I'll take Petra to the concert. What's the program for this evening?"

"Petra will not be going to any concert this night, or for that matter, any other night in the near future."

Doyle turned and blinked at Kagan. Kagan confronted him with a knowing smile. There was contempt in his eyes when he went on to say, "She's being put on trial."

"On trial? For *what?*" cried Doyle.

"As a security aide she left herself open to charges when she accompanied you out of range of the scanners."

"And who brought these charges against her—*you?*"

"Yes, sorry, old man. It was my sworn duty."

Doyle struggled to keep his anger under control. He drew a deep breath and peered at Kagan. "What could happen to her?"

Kagan did not expect such a question. He rather hoped Doyle would attack him in some way, perhaps even make a show of outrage. Quite flatly he said, "At most she could be sent to the work citadel. At least, she could be reprimanded and relieved of her rank. In any event, she will not be an aide any longer. She has forever lost that privilege."

"A security aide—a *privilege?*" Doyle laughed scoffingly.

"Yes, it is the highest privilege any citizen of 143 can ever hope to receive. It must be earned, as you shall soon be taught."

"You say she's being placed on trial. You speak as if she will be found guilty. What if she's found innocent?"

"That will not happen. The recordings are sufficient legal evidence that she breeched the regulations. You both were under scrutiny at the very moment you disobeyed the law and went into the water. You were observed deliberately evading the scanners."

Doyle smiled. He continued to peer contemptuously at Kagan. "This trial," he asked, "may I testify in her defense?"

"By all means. But you don't have to, you know."

"No, I didn't know. But I want to. She isn't guilty as you have charged. When is this trial to be conducted?"

"Within the hour. We deliver swift justice here."

"How efficient!" Doyle said. "And I gather you are her accuser *and* the prosecutor as well?"

"As a Secretariatist I am entitled to that honor."

"I am sure you are. Take me to her at once. That's an order."

Kagan bowed stiffly and waved Doyle to the exit. Doyle rose from the table without having touched his food. He strode through the automatic door and walked toward the transport tubes. "The second tube leads directly to the Justivac hall," Kagan called to him. "You'll find Petra there."

Doyle entered the second tube without pausing to see if Kagan was following or not. The door closed, and he was whisked through the transport network. Thirty seconds later the door opened, and he found himself in the corridor outside the great hall of the Justivac. He hurried to the entrance and showed the guards his unicard. They admitted him without question.

Doyle walked into the chamber toward Petra, who was standing to the right of the concordance keystone. High above them the whirling spheroid hummed and pulsated. When Petra saw him, a feeble smile came to her lips. He strode over to her and said, "I just heard. I want to testify on your behalf—to defend you."

"What's the use, darling?" she sighed. "The scanners don't lie. They saw us leave the surveillance area. Every move we made, every word we said has been recorded."

"So?"

"I'm guilty as charged."

"You intend to plead guilty?"

"Yes. The Justivac is programmed to be lenient on first offenders who admit their guilt."

Doyle grasped her by the shoulders. His hands tightened, and he bent to kiss her. As his lips touched hers, he said in a guarded whisper without moving his lips, "Plead not guilty. I have a plan."

They embraced, but her eyes were open, searching his. He tried to convey hope to her, to tell her it was important that she play it by ear and leave her defense up to him. When he released her, she smiled and gave him a subtle nod.

From above there came a great whirring sound like the rushing of whirling electrons in a cyclotron. Then a voice proclaimed, "Let the trial begin. Aide Petra, you are charged with knowingly evading surveillance. How do you plead?"

Petra, chewing her bottom lip, glanced toward Doyle. He nodded, and she gazed up at the spheroid. "I plead *not guilty*."

"Very well, then you are aware of the consequences if you should be found guilty?"

"I am."

"You are aware that a plea of guilty will get you a mandatory lenient sentence since this is your first offense against the state of Mnemosyne?"

"I am."

"And still you plead not guilty?"

"That is correct."

"Very well. Let it be duly recorded. The accused pleads not guilty. Are you prepared to offer a defense?"

"I am."

"Who will speak on your behalf?"

"Commandant Doyle."

"This is your final decision?"

"Yes, it is."

"Then proceed with the trial. Let the prosecutor step forward and the trial begin without further delay."

The door opened, and Kagan, in the company of two aides

109

marched in. They stopped just short of the concordanc keystone and saluted with their hands placed flat against the uniformed chests. "How say you, First Officer Kagan?"

"I accuse Aide Petra of willfully and knowingly disregar ing security by conducting Commandant Doyle to a place c rendezvous beyond the range of the state's scanners. Aid Petra is a security aide with the privilege of upholding securit I charge that she willfully and with malice usurped securit authority and placed Commandant Doyle's life in jeopardy i so doing. I ask the maximum penalty of this high court i order that other citizens will be discouraged from committin similar acts against the people of Mnemosyne."

"Very well," said the voice from the shimmering spheroi above. "Let the evidence be submitted."

A viewer was carried forward and placed to the right of th keystone by one of the aides who had accompanied Kagan. film revealed the images of Doyle and Petra as they wer through the labyrinth and then emerged at the edge of th pool. They saw and heard everything they had done and ever word they had uttered until they were out of the scannin range. They removed their footwear and went over the lo wall into the pool, then stepped into the deeper water an waded toward the waterfall where they vanished from sigh beyond the screen of water. Then the image showed th pictorial holograph of them. It faded out. Petra, whil watching the replay moved close to Doyle and grasped h hand. Her fingers tightened over his, and he could feel h trembling.

When the viewer was shut off after they had see themselves emerge from the waterfall and be taken int custody, the voice from above inquired, "First Officer Kaga do you wish to offer up any further evidence for th consideration of this court?"

"No, I do not. I stand on the grounds that what I hav shown is incriminating evidence, and I ask for the court to fin the defendant guilty as charged and sentence her to the maximum penalty as prescribed by law."

"Commandant Doyle," the voice from above said, "are you ready with your defense?"

"I am."

"Then proceed."

"I conclude that the court is satisfied that Aide Petra and I did this day go into the pool in the Gardens of Mnemosyne. Therefore, I should like to inquire of First Officer Kagan."

"You may proceed."

Doyle turned to Kagan. "Is it true that neither Aide Petra nor I could have left the pool at the base of the waterfall without again coming under surveillance?"

"Yes. That is correct."

"Is it true that the Gardens of Mnemosyne are so honeycombed with scanners that it is virtually impossible for anyone to get in or out without being scanned?"

"Yes, that is true. Security at the gardens is most efficient. Except for the area of the waterfall, the audiovisual scanners see and hear everything."

"Please tell the court, First Officer," Doyle said with clipped deliberation, "why is it that the audiovisual scanners cannot record or view the area in the vicinity of the waterfall?"

"The spraying water from the cascade splashes over the camera lenses and all that noise from the rushing torrent drowns out the sounds."

"Thank you, First Officer Kagan," Doyle said with a smile as he stood calmly beside Petra, his arm around her waist. "Now please answer my next question with a simple yes or no." He paused and smiled at Kagan, then asked, "To your knowledge, can you say whether or not the accused, Aide Petra, has any technical knowledge of the scanning devices used in the surveillance system, or if she has any knowledge whatsoever of devices, electronic or otherwise."

"To my knowledge she does not." He would not reply as Doyle asked.

"Would you say that Aide Petra is an enemy of the state?"

"To the best of my knowledge she is not."

"Please confine your answers to a simple yes or no."

"First Officer Kagan," the voice from above ordered, "you will reply in the manner by which the counsel for the defense has requested."

Kagan, his face coloring with suppressed anger, narrowed his eyes and watched Doyle. He was outwitted and he knew it.

"Now then," Doyle said, pacing about several steps and then hesitating a moment to brush off a bit of lint that had clung to his sleeve, "First Officer Kagan, does Aide Petra know anything at all about the operation of the scanners?"

"No."

"Since she knows nothing about the devices, therefore she could *not* have known the devices were inoperative in the vicinity of the waterfall. Is that correct?"

Kagan was burning with fury because of the line Doyle was taking and he had to reply in the affirmative, which he knew would topple his own case. "Yes."

At this, Doyle smiled and asked, "First Officer Kagan, please tell the court if, in your considered opinion, as an expert in security and a privileged member of the Secretariatist ranks, you believe that Aide Petra could possibly have known the devices were inoperative in the vicinity of the waterfall."

Kagan shifted his weight uneasily. He glared at Doyle and glanced upward at the shimmering spheroid. "No, I doubt if she knew that."

Doyle faced upward. "If it please the court, I should like to ask that charges against Aide Petra be dismissed and that new charges be placed against First Officer Kagan for attempting to use this high court for his own ends."

"I protest on the grounds that this is highly irregular and that Commandant Doyle is making a mockery of justice here."

"Silence, First Officer Kagan, that will be enough," said the voice from above. "On what grounds, Commandant Doyle, do you make such allegations?"

"I contend," Doyle said, "that First Officer Kagan was envious because Aide Petra accompanied me to the trysting place at the waterfall. He was envious because Aide Petra had formerly been his intimate companion and had broken off relations with him because she now finds affection for me. He quite knowingly and with malice attempted to use this court to satisfy his lust for vengeance. I therefore charge him with falsely accusing her of a crime against the state in order to take revenge. He knew only too well that Aide Petra and I could not have left the gardens at any time without again coming under the scanners. Therefore he has trumped up these charges only for his own selfish purposes."

There was a loud whirring from above, and then the spheroid descended several feet. The voice finally replied, "Charges against Aide Petra are hereby dismissed, since it has not been proved that she intentionally attempted to evade surveillance. As to the charges brought against First Officer Kagan, they will be taken under advisement. Such a procedure is highly irregular."

The spheroid ascended into the dome and the trial was over.

Petra, who had been listening intently to every word, exhaled and smiled with relief as Doyle gave her his hand and prepared to lead her out.

Kagan came forward, a dark expression on his face. His lip was curled downward as he said in a low voice, "Commandant Doyle, I demand to know why you're trying to have me removed from my post at the Orrery."

Doyle stopped short of the exit and laughed. "Whatever gave you that notion, Kagan?"

Kagan was not one to be trifled with. He glanced toward his two armed aides and said in a low voice, "Wait for me at the transport tubes." He waited until they were out of hearing and then replied, "I think I know what you're up to, Doyle. Mark my words, from this minute on I'll be watching you. I won't forget what you just tried to do to me. I think I'm on to you, and this is to assure you that I intend to arrest you the instant you step out of line."

"Doyle," Petra said, coming between them, "please don't feud because of this silly thing."

Doyle knew why she had interceded. She was playing up the angle of Kagan's jealousy to remove suspicion about Doyle and possible subversive activities. Kagan's jealousy and his ego were his own worst enemies, and Doyle knew he had to fear these most of all. He had made an enemy of Kagan and now he had to be doubly cautious, for he knew that Kagan had meant his threat—every word of it.

10

Decision

In answer to the summons from the hall of the Justivac, Petra and Doyle fell into step behind the servocourier and descended in the transport tube. When they arrived in the domed hall, they were not at all surprised to see Kagan already there standing beside the concordance keystone, shifting his weight from foot to foot. He did not look around when they came in, and he gave no sign of greeting. Petra smiled briefly up at Doyle and signaled with her glance that she was glad to see Kagan sweating for a change. During the past two days following their custodial arrest and detention prior to the trial, and Petra's acquittal after the brief hearing, they had not seen much of Kagan. Only when Doyle returned the next morning to spend the day in the Orrery on the bridge did he meet Kagan again; but Kagan was not speaking. He remained silent as they tested the circuits and ran the equipment in order to check the coordinates. Although the computer circuits were linked to the Orrery mechanism, it was still necessary to run tests and check the equations, making corrections and adjustments as they found them necessary. The complex was kept in a state of preparedness. This made Doyle extremely uneasy.

The shimmering spheroid above descended to within ten feet of their heads, and the voice announced, "First Officer

Kagan, we have taken under advisement the charges against you and feel they cannot be dismissed lightly. This is to reprimand you for your action; however, due to a technicality you are free to go. The technicality consists of an irregularity in the manner in which the charges were lodged against you during the trial of Aide Petra. From now on, First Officer Kagan, you are not to permit your personal feelings to sway your judgment or let them interfere with the quality of your work. It is within the realm of this court to command that you publicly apologize to Aide Petra and Commandant Doyle. So be it. You will now make your public apology."

Nothing could have vexed Kagan more. He turned, glaring angrily at Petra and Doyle. He swallowed audibly and then bowed his head. After a few moments of hesitation, he said, "Please accept my apologies for having inconvenienced the both of you."

Petra smiled and said, "Think no more about it, Kagan. You're forgiven."

Doyle made no reply. He stood there grinning at the humiliated Kagan.

Kagan eyed him with burning hatred. He said nothing more, turned, and started toward the exit. Doyle and Petra followed. When they reached the corridor, Doyle put his arm around Petra and called out to Kagan. "Just a moment, First Officer. Do you mind if we return to the waterfall? You see, we sort of like it there, and since our little dip was interrupted the other day, we might as well take up where we left off."

Kagan glared. He forced a smile and said, "No, I don't mind. But remember, next time you won't get away with it. Don't think for a moment that I'm not on to you."

"On to us—what is that supposed to mean?"

"Never mind. When I can prove it, I'll convict you. *That,* you may count on!"

Petra and Doyle descended to the transport level and took the scenic route around the city above ground, finally descending to the conveyor that led to the gardens. They barely spoke as they went through the labyrinth and then crossed to the waterfall. At the edge of the pool they removed their shoes and waded in. Then they dove into the water and cavorted for joy, splashing each other and laughing like children.

Doyle chased Petra until she was out of sight under the plunging cascade. They came up in the pool on the underside and Petra was quick to caution Doyle by saying, "We dare not go below now. We're being watched too closely."

"What about the camouflage?"

"I wish I knew. We must contact the kinsmen and let them know what's happening. The pictorial holograph must be out of order. And I suppose by now you want to see my grandfather concerning what new things you've learned about the Orrery complex?"

"You suppose right. It's imperative that I speak with him, even if only for a few minutes."

Petra floated around for a moment, then splashed some water in his face. "Tell you what. I'll swim around once, and you swim after me—pretend we're just playing around, playing tag or something like that. They'll not suspect anything. Then, the second time I go around I'll contact the door guards at the underground entrance and tell them to bring my grandfather up. We'll have to keep playing, going under the falls and out again so they'll believe we're really just having ourselves a bit of sport at Kagan's expense. Those watching will think that, I'm positive."

Doyle nodded. "Then let's go."

Petra swam away and vanished under the tumbling waters. She came up on the other side and continued swimming, making a circuit of the frothing waters, then when Doyle appeared, she taunted him and dove beneath the surface. He took off in pursuit. Several passersby ashore stopped and smiled.

Doyle came up on the underside of the waterfall and saw Petra in the water, speaking to one of the sentries who had been posted inside the camouflaged door. The man nodded and the door quickly closed after him. Petra swam away once more, and they slowly paddled through the waterfall again. By the time they made their third circuit, Petra motioned to Doyle that her grandfather was waiting to speak to him. Doyle crossed to the doorway, and a gray-haired man with a round face emerged.

"Commandant Boden?"

"You are Doyle," Boden said with an approving smile. "Don't worry, we are monitoring the outside area of the waterfall pool. So far no one suspects what you are up to. If anything, they believe you and Petra are having a lark just to nettle Kagan. However, you will not be able to come here too often. They're suspicious but so far haven't found the secret doorway. And by the way, before we go to other matters, let me warn you about Kagan. He's nobody's fool. He's a menace and a diabolical one at that."

Doyle smiled. "That's right, you should know him and his ways. He was your first officer when you were Orrery commandant."

"He was one of the major reasons why I defected and permitted the kinsmen to make my disappearance appear to be a tragic accident. Most of us in the underground are allegedly dead anyway, so we have to be particularly cautious. If we're caught by agents of the Secretariat, there'll be no mercy. Since we're supposed to be dead anyway, they will have nothing to lose by murdering us."

"How extensively do you have the Orrery complex and the other citadels bugged with sensors?" Doyle asked.

Boden thought a moment and replied, "Not too well, I'm afraid. All we've managed to do is tap the Secretariat's monitoring fields. But whenever classified material is brought out or secret meetings conducted, scrambling fields are set up and we cannot pick up anything of use. Incidentally, how did you get on during your first day in the Orrery complex up on the bridge?"

"It was an awesome experience," Doyle said. "Frightening to think that all that power is at one's fingertips—one like Kagan and perhaps others like him in the Secretariat."

"Now you understand why I secretly constructed my sanctum—and now you know why I defected. Since I couldn't fight them singlehandedly, I had to join up with the others. I made them aware of what we're fighting. Together we will overcome them."

"What can I do?" Doyle asked, his expression intent, his gaze fixed on the elder man's wrinkled face.

"I cannot answer that. I tried any number of things, but nothing seemed to work. Sabotage of the dynamotor system will only delay what they are up to. Besides, you are constantly watched, and you would be arrested immediately if you tried anything like that."

"Which was why you built your atomic clock. How on earth did you manage that?"

Boden smiled gravely. "It took years of pilfering the parts I needed to build the clock. That was the hardest part—handling the isotope after I stole it from one of the cyclotrons. Gave myself a potentially fatal dose of radiation poisoning as the result; but thanks to Dr. Joyko, my condition was arrested, and my health remains status quo."

"And how did you complete the circuit to the clock? How did you manage that?"

"I tunneled through the walls into the isolation space between the floors. But I'm an old man, and I don't think the shielded cables were attached close enough down to the dynamotors. According to my calculations the cables should be within three wavelengths—"

"The floor space you spoke about?" Doyle interrupted. "Can you tell me how far one can go?"

Boden smiled. "I was unable to explore them deep enough or high enough. I believe that if you climb up to the upper level on par with the Justivac hall in the adjacent citadel, you could make it across to the Secretariat's chambers."

"But you're not certain?"

"No. There's an outside chance however, that you might turn up the cable harness connecting the Orrery consoles to the remote console in the Secretariat's chambers."

"Are you certain they possess such a device?"

"Absolutely. As you know, they monitor everything said and done in the Orrery, especially the bridge. A few months before I defected, I discovered that I could not activate several of the switches. While I was behind the console checking the circuitry, I located patch lines embedded in the construction. Those patch lines led down through the walls and into the floor space. Later I observed some of the controls apparently being manipulated from somewhere other than the bridge—which led me to the conclusion that such a remote console panel *does* exist—and most likely in the Secretariat's chambers."

Doyle was lost in thought for several moments. Finally he collected the cluttered bits of data in his mind and asked, "If I do locate the console, what then? How do I go about deactivating or neutralizing it?" He paused and then added, "Since the circuitry is embedded in the construction, it would be virtually impossible to get to it that way."

"I thought of that many times. Even if you managed somehow to take cutting torches into the inner floor, you still would not be able to cut through the construction material deep enough to sever the wiring. No, the only way is to find the remote console panel and sabotage the system from there. If they can be immobilized that way, and if you can then get to the Justivac's memory banks and do some programming of your own, we would then be able to chop off the brain and dismantle the enemy of our state without shedding a drop of blood."

"Do you know they've militarized dozens of servomen?"

"Yes. Actually thousands. They've been programmed to—I hate to say it—slaughter every human being in sight when given the order."

"Who can press that button?"

"How did you guess it was a button?"

"I surmised as much. I noticed several of the armed guards around Kagan. They were wearing curiously shaped skull caps. I've seen similar-shaped caps on cybernetized subhumans, some of whom were sent to experiment stations in the frontiers. I was told the medics were experimenting with electronic control mechanisms in the human brain, purportedly to cure the hopelessly insane, schizoids and paranoids, for instance. I didn't buy that, but whatelse could I do except sound off?"

"It's fortunate for you we were able to intercept many of the dossier reports before they were fed into the Justivac; otherwise, you might never have been recalled and placed in my former post."

Doyle grinned. "How did you know that I was the one to fill your shoes?"

Boden nodded and glanced toward Petra, who was swimming around again. She waved to them, and Boden lifted his hand and waved to her. "That's your answer," he said, nodding toward her.

Doyle turned and grinned at Petra. She paused and playfully squirted a mouthful of water toward him. Then she swam away again, vanishing in the water as though the churning foam had swallowed her.

"I want to thank you, Doyle, for the clever way you defended Petra and obtained her freedom and reinstatement," Boden said. "I'm indebted to you for that. It shows she wasn't wrong about your capabilities, and I believe that if anyone can bring off our coup, you are the one man who can."

"Which brings us to a discussion of our ultimate plan," Doyle said. "What happens once I neutralize the Orrery complex?"

"We move against them."

"In force."

"Hardly. First the servomen must be immobilized. We must find out who controls them; who in the Secretariat is empowered to push the button."

"Have you any idea who that may be?"

"Not the slightest. If we knew, our plan could be laid and everything would be simplified. But how can you blueprint a strategy when you don't even know whom you're fighting or where they may be found? For all we know, they may be located nowhere near the great hall of the Justivac."

"Then the Justivac may provide the key."

"Perhaps, but that is the most closely guarded and sensor-monitored citadel on the planet. It would be far too risky for you to venture in there. The access areas, which were all sealed after construction was completed, have also been boobytrapped for an extra precaution."

"Are you certain?"

"Yes. A dozen of our men went in and never came out again. So far as we were able to determine, they were disintegrated. I wouldn't want you to attempt that."

"But the Justivac citadel may be the only weak link in the chain."

Boden nodded, rejecting this idea before Doyle could go further with it. "What good will you be to yourself or to us if you are dead?"

"But some way must be found to get into the Justivac citadel to get to the memory banks and reprogram them. Isn't there some way in that you may have overlooked?"

"I'm afraid not. You'll have to devise some other method."

"How will I let you or the kinsmen know? Do you want Petra or myself to return here?"

For the present, I would say that would be unwise. There is one other place we may rendezvous without being overheard, however. It is in the main amphitheater. As Orrery commandant you are entitled to your own reserved loge. We will have a cable there to which you may attach this miniature microphone."

"But won't I be overheard?"

Boden smiled. "Not at all, provided you speak to us during the music. Tonight, for instance, the Firebird Suite is scheduled on the program. The orchestra will make it impossible to monitor you over the audio sensors. They will have to content themselves to observe you visually. If you sit with your head close to Petra's after the fashion of lovers," he paused to chuckle and wink, "Kagan and his masters will think only you're cooing in your lovebird's ear. Only in dire emergency will you or Petra ever return here again."

"Isn't there some other access to your underground complex?"

"Yes, there are many points of access. But for the present, they are sealed at the base of each transportation tube. When the time is ripe, one thousand of us will invade Mnemosyne and take the city in one fell swoop. But everything will have to be timed to the split second. We await your signal. The moment you have neutralized the Orrery and deactivated the servomen, we will move."

"That's a tall order," Doyle said, shivering more from the staggering task that lay ahead than from the chill water he was standing in.

"You're a tall man," Boden said, moving toward the secret door. "We'll be praying for you, Doyle. Good luck."

"I didn't think there were people left in the universe who prayed any more."

Boden smiled. Then he disappeared beyond the granite

door, and it swung shut, sealing him in, leaving Doyle alone with his thoughts.

The time was drawing near for action, he knew; and just as Boden said, it was all up to him, for he was the kinsmen's sole link with the outside. Doyle paddled through the water and rejoined Petra. Before they returned to the other side of the pool through the tumbling cascade of frothing water, she kissed him lightly on the mouth and inquired, "Did you arrange a method of keeping in touch with the kinsmen?"

"Yes," he grinned at her. "How would you like to go to the concert tonight?"

"I'd love it—especially if you'll put your arm around me and rest your head on my shoulder."

Doyle blinked at her in surprise. "How did you know?"

"I can read lips, darling," she laughed.

He seized her roughly and held her fast. "If you can read lips—then so will the others be able to do so if we're being monitored during the concert visually."

"Silly," Petra said, "all you have to do is teach yourself to speak *without* moving your lips. It's easy, once you practice a little." She laughed up at him and bussed him on the nose. "Now say you love me without moving your lips."

"I love you."

"No, you moved your lips. Try it next time by biting on your bottom lip. Go on, try it."

Doyle held his bottom lip between his teeth. "I love you," he said. Then he burst into laughter. "It really works."

"Of course it does," she said. "Where do we go from here?"

He swam beside her toward the shore. "I have work to do in the Orrery. Now that we've had our fun, darling, shall we be off?"

11

Command

For two hours before he returned to his quarters where Petra awaited him to take her to the concert, Doyle worked in the Orrery, logging population center coordinates on the daily journal sheet. It was a painstaking task, keeping track of the citizens on the planet. The routine, which Kagan had informed him was the commandant's responsibility, was rather mundane and trivial. It seemed to Doyle that a high-ranking commandant had more important administrative matters to see to than performing a mere clerk's duty. On the other hand, after he reconsidered what had to be done, there was actually little else for him to do. The computers checked out within a few minutes. After that the Orrery complex was activated and the mockup put into motion across the domed ceiling.

Laser tracers marked the positions, minutes, degrees, and azimuths of every human being on Pulsar 143 so there was little else to be done except make an occasional minor adjustment. When it came down to activating the ion bands, or attempting anything with the console that had to do with the weapon, he knew he did not dare venture near the dials or switches, for to do so would bring disaster to himself and all hope for the kinsmen would be lost.

He went about his tasks slowly, deliberately, alert to every detail of the Orrery bridge. He searched for some clue, some hint that might provide him with the way to engineer a neutralization of the complex. It was horrible to think that just the touch of a button could make a slave out of every human being.

Kagan entered shortly before 2000 hours and relieved Doyle at the bridge. He came into the vast control area and went right to the log sheet that was mounted on a bulkhead beside the main window, which overlooked the huge dynamos in the vaulted ceilinged hall beyond and below. For nearly six hundred feet straight down to the dimly lighted catwalks, the enormous reactor-driven power plants and ion drivers could be seen maintaining a steady power ratio that fed the turbines in another section of the complex.

Doyle understood enough about the Orrery device to know that it would take several days to build up enough energy to activate the weapon, if that was the proper name for the device. As long as all systems appeared to be humming steadily without an increase in the power levels he knew all was well. But the moment there was a shift in the levels, it would be time to start worrying, and perhaps then it would be too late.

He decided not to risk questioning Kagan, who would not tell him anything even if his life depended on it—of *that*, Doyle was certain. Therefore, he had to remain alert and watch Kagan at all times, observing everything he did and everything he did not do.

With this in mind, and with the knowledge that he would need lots of time and patience in order to see this thing through, Doyle left the bridge and went to fetch Petra.

Fifteen minutes later they were in the reserved loge at the amphitheater waiting for the symphony to begin the evening program. Petra kept her conversation trivial during the time they were waiting for the first selection to be played. As soon as the conductor began and the orchestra's music filled the amphitheater, she said holding the inside of her bottom lip between her teeth to keep it still, "Did you accomplish anything?"

"No."

"You're not giving up?"

"I wouldn't dream of it." He paused and found the audio cable protruding from the seat. He fitted the tiny microphone to it and then put his arm around Petra. "I've nothing but this to report. On the bridge everything is as per usual. Nothing out of the ordinary. I logged the positions of eighteen colonies we did not know existed here. The underground citadel and all personnel are undetectable—thank God! I made some adjustments. Nothing else was corrected. Kagan arrived without saying anything to me and proceeded to go about the routine of checking the power levels and then the Orrery coordinates. We didn't speak. I searched for some way to take action but could find none. I'll advise you when I turn something up. In the meantime, I'd like a backpack and coveralls of insulated material sent to my quarters. If you can manage that, please include a power light and tools. Give me whatever you think I might need for exploring the innerwalls and floors of the complex. I may require powerful laser cutters too, something strong enough to lase through plastic cement six feet thick. Also try to obtain a set of blueprints of the citadel and the Justivac hall, something that shows the probable layout of the scanning network and the circuitry of the Orrery complex. I know this is a tall order, but I need it if I'm to stand tall for all of us."

"What's that supposed to mean?" Petra said when Doyle removed the minimike and restored it to his cuff pocket.

Doyle pecked her on the cheek and whispered, "Maybe someday I'll tell you."

"Darling," she whispered, glancing around to see if they were being overheard. The music was filling the air, and no one in the nearby loges seemed to be looking their way.

"Yes?" he said, anticipating what she was about to say.

127

"Can I help?"

"You can—by staying put. Tonight I'm going into the sanctum and then through it. Your grandfather told me of a possible route to the hall of the Justivac. If this is to be a bloodless coup, and if we are to succeed without bringing death and destruction down on our heads and the rest of mankind out there in space—I've got to find the way. God help me, I've got to."

"Then take me with you. I'm in good physical condition. I can do all sorts of things that'll surprise you. I can climb—use tools, weapons, and read schematics."

"I don't doubt that you can. But I'll need you to cover for me in my absence."

She smiled at him, her eyes gleaming. "Then I am to pretend that I'm your mistress?"

"Yes."

"That should tie Kagan in emotional knots."

"I'm counting on that too," he said. "It might be just the thing to get him to show his Achilles heel."

"Huhnh?"

"If he loses his self-control, as I think he will, there's no telling what he'll do. I think he might try something drastic like framing us for something we didn't do, or perhaps if he's provoked enough, he might even send a couple of his servoguards to kill me."

Petra gasped. "He wouldn't!"

"He just might. I've been watching Kagan, and I think I have my finger on what makes him tick. He's an egomaniac. He can't stand the shock of losing you to me. Now he must prove he's superior to me. It isn't that I think he loves you, or loves anybody, or is even capable of loving anyone. It's just that he craves gratification for his ego needs and will probably stop at nothing to achieve that gratification, even if it brings about his own destruction."

"You really think that, don't you? You're not just guessing."

"I've studied human nature for too many years not to know what I'm talking about, Petra. Kagan doesn't love you and never has. He loves himself. He must prove to himself that he's a better man than I am. He must therefore discredit me and destroy me. Then he can save face by telling you—after he believes I'm out of the way permanently—that he doesn't want you after all."

"That sounds crazy and mixed up."

"It is just that, and so is this whole diabolical new order. The tragedy of it all is that a handful of madmen have somehow managed to seize power and gain control of this entire planet. They've managed this through chicanery and subterfuge, by subverting our freedoms and turning our free states into police states. It's the very thing that led me to join the first space pioneers back in '83 when we were fed up with the way the world was going. We wanted a new life in a new world that would be free of all the evils of the past; we needed a system of government that would be the antithesis to those systems of our native earth."

"You've been here a mere seventeen years and I a lifetime, as my father, and his father before him. It seems incredible that our times are different and yet we are here together, now, fighting for this same thing."

"Fighting?" Doyle said. "This isn't the correct word. In my lexicon only one word can describe what we are attempting here and now, Petra. Just as I age one year for every thirty that you age, so all this will come to pass and eventually a new government and a new way of life will arise in its place. Perhaps your children's children will one day enjoy all that we labor for here and now."

"I'd like that to be *our* children's children," she said, rather wistfully, her eyes gazing at him with adoration.

Doyle nodded. "Petra, my dear, I won't discuss such matters. You are but a child. I am of those who number less than two hundred now—and we are the ageless young men—those who are more or less self-appointed to right the

129

wrongs man has committed against other man. I can't help it, but that's the way it is. I would have been dead eons ago had it not been for that trajectory fluke during the first flight on Pilgrimage II when the nuclear reactors went haywire and we were rifled past the speed of light, only to return and find that time as well as all things had made us different from all the others, different from you—and forced us to reside in a different time span."

"Shh," she whispered, touching his lips as the symphonic composition drew to a close.

They arose when the crowds arose and departed the way the crowds departed, through the exits into the malls and down the conveyor transports to the cubicles. Overhead, high above the domed city, the six roons glowed ruddy and pink-red like six bleary bloodshot eyes staring down at them. Doyle and Petra walked hand in hand along one of the walkways overlooking the citadels of the city. Beyond, in the artificial light of the sentry satellites orbiting the planet just above the distant horizon, they saw rainbows of light as the redshift spectrum in its height blossomed forth and illuminated the entire galactic triad.

"Isn't it a spellbinding sight?" Petra whispered when they paused to rest and stare at the phenomena.

"I'd rather not say," he grinned down at her. "Shouldn't we be getting back?"

Petra giggled and hugged him tightly. She had him, but she knew she did not possess him. Their romance was a sham; a fraud; merely a coverup for what Doyle had to do. She wished it could be different, and then decided wishing was no good. Reality was all that mattered. She would try to remember that.

For the benefit of the scanners, Doyle and Petra stopped and embraced several times. When they finally arrived at the quarters at the Orrery citadel, Doyle led Petra into his bed chamber. He held her closely and after they embraced, switched off the lights. Then he drew her down to the sonic bed and activated the fields. He understood enough about the sensor system and the scanner mechanisms to know that once the sonic bed was activated the scanners were inoperative. But the moment the sonic bed was vacated, the scanners switched on again. This was the last vestige of privacy accorded the people of 143.

The moment they were in bed together, Doyle pressed his hand to Petra's lips and explained, "You must remain here—in bed—until I return. If both of us get out of this sonic field, the scanners will alert Kagan that I'm not here. Now can you do that, Petra? Will you stay here and wait for me—no matter how long I'm gone?"

She nodded and he released his hold over her lips. Then he kissed her lightly, and slipped out of bed. He crept through the darkened bed chamber and went into the bath, softly closing the door after him. In the darkness he knelt down and groped for the nodule on the sink pipe. He located it and opened the sanctum, then slipped through and closed it after him, finding, to his delight, the backpack he had requested. Fastened to the neatly strapped bundle was a note. Doyle unfolded the paper and grinned at the message that was signed by Boden. Boden stated simply that he had programmed Nanny, his former servomaid, to obey him without question. It was she who had delivered the parcel, which the kinsmen had smuggled into the galley and then sneaked to her for delivery.

Doyle was amused to think that a servomaid could be entrusted with such a task. On the other hand, he was not at all amused to think that the success of the undertaking as well as the lives of all concerned depended on one subhuman servowoman. The thought that she could be compelled to betray them all was unnerving. Doyle was not thinking of himself. He was thinking, instead, of Petra and the hundreds of people who had found their way to the underground quarters of the kinsmen.

During the years that he had been content to remain on the frontier, Doyle had no idea that the free people of Mnemosyne had little by little surrendered all of their freedoms until they now had become total nonentities within the confines of a concentration camp that looked like a modern city. He wondered now what might have happened if he had exercised the initiative to return to the city he had helped found to put a stop to what was happening. Could he have managed then to achieve that end?

He smiled and remembered something of the history of earth and its great civilizations. He recalled the downfall of America, how the people refused to believe they were being destroyed by enemies from within, fellow travelers who aided and abetted that nation's traitors, until it was too late to stop the divisiveness, the destruction of all its great institutions. Just as no one then listened to the warnings of those few dedicated patriots who were bold and brave enough to stand and protest against what was happening and beg for support, so no one on Pulsar 143 would have heeded his warnings had he returned to Mnemosyne. Now that they had lost their freedoms and were mere vassals of a feudal Secretariat whose police state controlled the very air they breathed, now it was too late.

Or *was* it too late? wondered Doyle as he strapped on the backpack and found the hole in the wall that Boden had carved out. At least Boden had done everything he could do then and was wise enough to go underground and join those seeking to overthrow the tyrants who had taken power. Now it was Doyle's chance, and he was determined to succeed.

Despite his determination, he also knew that even if he succeeded in doing the impossible, once the people of 143 were free again and their civil liberties restored, they would soon forget the tyrants who had imprisoned them and would be ripe for it to happen all over again. At first they would become derelict in their duties to themselves and their country by neglecting to vote. Then evil men would rise to power on the pretext they were honest and kind and just. Before long they would be firmly lodged in positions of high office where they would remain solely because the people did not care to vote them out of office; or, for that matter, they would remain in power because the people did not care enough to vote. Once this happened, a new and different order would abolish the old order and a new brand of tyranny would rule the planet.

Knowing this, Doyle went through the hole in the wall and began to creep along a ledge sixty stories above the ground. "Why am I risking my neck?" he asked himself. Then he laughed. He laughed because he told himself that maybe this time, on this planet so far away from mother earth, man would learn the lesson of history and then apply what he had learned in order to sanctify his existence and build a better world for his progeny.

12

Search

The rooms within the rooms upon the wall upon which the order of memory was built were not too different from the inner walls of the citadel, which Doyle painstakingly ascended in his climb to the top of the dome above the Orrery complex. Sinking winds roared down from the outer reaches of the domed city, and he had to stuff his ears with bits of cloth in order to keep his sanity and continue his search. When the city had originally been constructed, it was erected in stages beneath the great plasma dome that was jacked higher and higher on the four citadels. When the weathersphere was erected, the sinking winds were deflected, and it became possible for man to tame the countryside to the outer reaches of the suburban moors. Beyond that, once man learned to build deflectors, he was able to explore the strange surrealistic world of Pulsar 143. Hence, Doyle had grown accustomed to the privations and hardships of living on this alien planet and had consequently taught others how to survive. After a network of deflectors had been erected and satellites placed into orbit that reflected sunlight to the polar caps and began the slow melting process that provided water, colonies were started in all hemispheres and man survived and flourished. But since the coming of the new order, first in Mnemosyne, the capital city, and later in the cities of the muses, all that had changed. Now it was up to him to find a way to restore freedom, and he felt confident that the key was somewhere within the citadel over which he was climbing.

He had memorized the principal workings of the Orrery complex and hoped to find somewhere on that dizzy height a traceable circuit, a clue by which he might be led to the secret control panel. Clinging to the top of the dome for dear life Doyle inched along in the murky darkness, feeling his way clawing for handholds, groping for the circuit harness that he was certain had to be there. He had made almost a complete circuit of the five hundred yard hemisphere atop the dome when he suddenly located it. A tubular harness emerged from directly above the place where he judged the console on the Orrery bridge to be located. It led downward in a straight line. Hand over hand he clung to it until he reached the ledge at the exact equator of the dome, high above the chasm below. As he rested a moment, his body flat against the giant orb, he could feel the humming vibration of the mighty power plants, and he knew he was directly above them, shielded from their radiation by a six-foot-thick layer of plasmatized cement. He did not dare think of what would happen if he lost his bearing and could not find his way back to the hole in the wall; he did not dare think about the sudden death he would meet if he fell from that tremendous height. Instead, he concentrated on one thing—tracing the cable harness to its terminus.

After lowering his backpack a trifle so he could reach into it without losing his balance on the narrow ledge joining the top of the dome to the vertical sides of the citadel tower structure, he found the small searchlight he had been seeking. He turned it on and played the beam along the cable harness. It was seemingly endless, stretching down from the dome and across the abyss for about fifty yards where it was affixed to a second, smaller dome. Doyle did not hesitate. He knew time was against him. He made certain his backpack was secure then pocketed the searchlight and descended to the ledge where the cable ran outward. He got a firm grip with both hands and lowered himself down. Slowly but surely he ventured across, counting as he made his way, making a game of it, seeing if he could guess how many yards he had to go. Moreover, he wanted to be certain of the distance because he would need to return that way, and it was important to keep that in mind.

When he reached the opposite side and gained a foothold on the ledge of the second citadel tower top, he slumped there until he caught his breath. He had no idea his arms would be so tired or that he would feel so drained of energy. He nibbled at an energy stick and almost at once felt his strength return. He removed the light and continued the dangerous task of tracing the cable. It snaked around the dome in an almost helter-skelter manner, as though those who had installed it were so afraid of slipping to their deaths that they had failed to do a tidy job. He smiled at this thought and played the handlight over the cable. It terminated at an opening that had been sealed with a large plate that had in turn been sealed by a pliant gasket. Doyle settled himself above the plate, which covered an opening large enough to climb through, provided the plate could be pried loose, and with several of the tools in the backpack, he began to cut away the gasket. After a few minutes he had removed enough of the material to enable him to see downward into the citadel dome. He seemed to be above a chamber of sorts. In the center of the chamber, beside a lighted console panel, was a master viewer. Ten rows of ten screens each could be seen. From the top of the dome where he was, Doyle could not distinguish the views being monitored. He broke away more of the material and then pried the manhole-sized plate free. Then he climbed through it, clinging with one arm wrapped around the cable as he descended several feet and then repositioned the plate above, so his presence would not be discovered. The cable was attached to the underside of the dome. He followed it down, moving slowly, hand over hand. When he reached the side of the wall about twenty feet above the floor, he looked around, saw no one present, and hurriedly completed his descent.

Resting a moment behind one of the consoles, he peered at the viewing screens and tried to orient himself. He decided he was in the Secretariat chambers above the Justivac spheroid. The thought occurred to him that he was getting very close to his goal. Now the question was—what ought he do? He could not go back to his quarters without being found out. Since he was this far and had infiltrated the Justivac complex, he decided to continue his search before choosing a plan. Before he could act, he would need to know everything possible about the Secretariat and the things they were doing. He would need a safe place to hide until he could make his move, and no place within the limits of the City of Mnemosyne was any safer than in the very complex occupied by the Secretariat, for his sensor detector, which the kinsmen had also included in the backpack, indicated that no devices of that sort were anywhere in evidence. Breathing a sigh of relief, Doyle left the central area and began to explore the apartments beyond the console area.

To the right and above the sphere in which the readout and voice units of the Justivac were located was a locked and sealed strong door. From the size, thickness, and shape of it, Doyle knew what was beyond—the Justivac's memory banks. He examined the locks and saw that three keys were required to open it. This was obviously a security measure to prevent any one person from entering alone, ensuring that three persons—each with one of the keys—would enter together.

Doyle went to the adjacent chambers and found himself in a file room containing dossiers of Mnemosyne citizens. He scanned the files of dossier cubes and stopped abruptly when he saw that the files contained facts on individuals suspected of wanting to overthrow the Secretariat. Doyle was staggered the size of the dossier collection. It seemed to contain the names of the majority of citizens in residence in the community. The purpose of that file room being there adjacent to the master scanner viewers brought a chill to his heart. He wondered if the members of the Secretariat, whoever they were, would make the same reply as did Kagan when he had asked, "Who was Hitler?" Again and again, Doyle had seen history repeat itself. He was weary of it and growing wearier by the hour.

He tightened the cinch holding the backpack and crept silently toward the next door. He peered inside and realized it was a galley. In the gloom he saw servomaids standing against the wall and sitting at tables, staring absently, blank-eyed, awaiting the time to reactivate and go about the duty of fulfilling another day's program.

The next doorway led to a small but lavishly furnished apartment. Asleep in a sonic bed was a man whom Doyle recognized as Abbott, one of the trio who had met him on the stage on behalf of the Secretariat when he was publicly promoted to commandant. He stared at the snoring man, then stole away and returned to the central area where he then approached the next door. Inside was the man who was called Bailey. Suddenly Doyle had an idea. He crept into the bed chamber and rummaged through the slumbering man's effects until he found the great metallic key and examined the chain to which it had been linked. He removed the key and returned to Abbott's bed chambers. After a thorough search, he found Abbott's key concealed in his right shoe. He removed it and stole out again, proceeding toward the third bed chamber. Just as he expected, he recognized the occupant as Cecil, the third person who had been in the presentation ceremony.

Once the keys were in his possession, Doyle swiftly made a circuit of the other apartments ringing the consoles and when he was confident no one else was about, he went straight toward the memory bank vaults to the Justivac. He unlocked the door with the three keys and stepped inside, quickly shutting the door after him, then relocking it so he would not be disturbed. He found himself in a vast room containing countless thousands of mems arranged in row after row of tiny gray cubes, pushed into sockets that connected them to the network of circuitry. He removed his backpack and searched everywhere for a schematic of the chambers and finally had to give it up because he could find no clues anywhere to the way it operated. He decided that the Justivac had been programmed to remember its own schematic layout and then tried to determine how to get it to reveal it. He went to the readout console at the extreme end of the vault and sat at the lighted panel, studying the nomenclature system.

He knew that the mind code had been programmed into the electron brain, but he did not know which keys should be depressed to bring forth the answer. He decided to go back through the mem banks and look for some key to the filing system. As he went along playing his handlight over the cubes he finally saw it. A system of corresponding nomenclature was evident. Then the entire network took on meaning. He returned to the readout panel and asked the machine by punching the keys, "How are you nomenclatured?"

There was a faint hum, and the keys began to click. "Decimal system glyphs. Cubes contain data all classifications. Cite classifications wanted and Justivac will reply with flip-flop delivery. Schematic readout available."

Doyle was jubilant at his good fortune. He asked the machine to deliver up the schematics and it did so. Then he asked it for a schematic of the scanning network throughout Mnemosyne. It delivered it before he could blink. He tore off the parchment and stared. To his excitement he discovered it was all incredibly simple. Then he smiled to himself. He saw that a feeder of data was supplied in each of the bed chambers of the three men whom he had just visited.

Without pausing to set the machine in motion again, he left

he memory banks and returned to the central console room. He entered the bed chambers of the three men one after one, located the phone pads, and stealthily clamped each pad to their beds. Then he depressed the brain wave oscillator and set the receptors on output. He hurriedly returned to the memory bank, reclosed the door and locked it after him, and went to the schematic chart and began depressing readout cubes. This fed the stored mems into the stimulator circuits that in turn fed the data directly to the three slumbering men. Doyle grinned. He knew his idea would work, for he had once used a similar process to educate himself while he slept. He went along the banks, selecting by consulting the charts the areas of knowledge that he knew would serve to change the thinking of the three men whom he had placed in arrested sleep.

Then Doyle rummaged through one of the lockers behind the readout panel and withdrew a hand case containing programming receptors. He left the memory banks with the Justivac still humming and entered the galley where the deactive servomaids were standing and sitting. He fixed a receptor to the ear of each servo and once again returned to the memory banks. He fed question after question into it and when he at last had all the answers he needed, he proceeded to the next phase of his plan. He studied the blueprints of the scanning system and after some careful computations, figured out how and where to overload the circuitry and cause a total blackout. He went to the console area and stood before the master viewer, punching the keys, searching for Kagan. He then struck the coordinates 772 which were the composite of the name Kagan, and to his amazement found that he had guessed correctly. Kagan was seen in the central scope slowly resetting the switches on the Orrery activator.

At this, Doyle's hair stood on end. Kagan was energizing the ion fields! He leaned forward and brought the viewing tubes in closer so he might read the power level indicators. What he saw made his insides turn over. The throbbing meters were rapidly beginning to rise above the test level toward the activation levels. Once they were beyond the -0 gauges and in the +0 scales, it would be too late.

He rushed back to the computer and punched out several questions. The replies were delivered instantly. Then he made several rapid calculations and gave the Justivac a command. He sought to neutralize Kagan's efforts by draining off the power reserves that were building up. Then he rushed out and began to search the area thoroughly, hunting for the master console that governed the Orrery complex. He had failed to locate it upon entering the Secretariat's chambers and for the moment had neglected to finish tracing the cable harness he had followed from the Orrery complex. Suddenly he saw what he had overlooked. The cable, which ran downward from the dome overhead, was nearly camouflaged as it went behind the consoles and appeared to descend into the floor. He ran to it and located a hidden trapdoor. He probed the area with his sensor wand and listened for the clicks, which finally came indicating a switch was near at hand. He located the concealed secret switch and touched it. At once the master console began to lift up from beneath hidden panels in the floor. It was surrounded by viewers that revealed every inch, every switch and every dial on the Orrery bridge. With hands shaking from excitement, Doyle neutralized the energizing switch relays and hastily began to shut down every system Kagan had activated.

Then on the viewers he saw Kagan stop what he was doing and glare upwards, shouting at the top of his voice, "You fools! Why are you turning against me? Don't you know it's too late? Have you forgotten we've decided to go through with it, and I've already bypassed these controls?"

At those words, Doyle stiffened. Could it be, he wondered, that Kagan was telling the truth? If so, how could he shut down the amassing energy pile? He knew now that every second counted; that it might be only a few minutes or at most a few scant hours before it would be too late to halt the buildup except by bringing about the self-destruction of the entire energy mass by triggering Boden's atomic clock.

Doyle once again fled to the computer and frantically began to punch out question after question. The computer replied to each question instantly. At last Doyle had exhausted his ideas and was at a loss to know what to do, except for one final thing, there *was* something to be done!

He returned to the scanner and saw Kagan calmly going about the task of resetting the dials and switches on the Orrery bridge. Then he depressed the command buttons 04832 and scanned the servoguards' regimental headquarters. He watched the servos come to life and march rapidly to the central assembly room. When they were all gathered and standing at attention in long ranks, Doyle picked up the microphone and gave the command, "Stand easy. Activate cyclonders to the maximum at destruct levels. Now each man face his partner." He paused and watched through the widescreen viewer as eighteen thousand servoguards turned right and left in ranks facing each other. He swallowed with some difficulty and clenched his hands. He did not relish what he was about to do, but it was important first to immobilize the forces at Kagan's beck and call.

"Take aim with your weapons and point them at each others' chests. When I give the command to fire, you will fire."

He hesitated again, breaking out in a cold sweat. Then he said, "*Fire!*"

There was a dazzling spectacle of blazing light, and before his eyes the entire army of servoguards disintegrated.

Doyle was sweating profusely. He did not enjoy what he had just done. The servos were subhuman, but that still did not mean what he had done was right. He knew they had been programmed to annihilate the citizens of 143, so they had had to be destroyed.

Doyle tried once again to think of some way to stop the energy pile Kagan had activated. He knew of no way. Then he lifted his left hand and depressed the communicator emblem on his ring, touching the tiny buttons reading out ex-commandant Boden's call numerals.

A moment later he heard Boden's voice. "This is 912."

"This is Doyle," he said tersely. "I'm in the dome above the hall of the Justivac. I've immobilized the Secretariat and incinerated the servoarmy, but so far I've been unable to stop Kagan. He's already begun the activation of the energy pile."

"Have you located the master console?" Boden asked.

"I have, but it doesn't respond. The buildup is already approaching the azimuth."

"How far from the plus-zero power level readings?"

"Six spaces and closing fast."

"Oh, my God!" Boden whispered.

"Tell me what to do!" Doyle cried. "Think man! There *must* be a way."

13

Concordance

Boden finally found the answer. His voice came over the minispeakers dry and crisp, terse with apprehension. "Yes, I believe there *is* a way. The concordance keystone. If you can find the program cube used to program Kagan's mind, you might find the answer there. I know of no other way."

Doyle rushed back into the memory bank and with shaking hands traced the circuitry. Then he located the proper numeral sequences and depressed the switches. He ran along the rows and rows of cube banks until at last he saw the one he was seeking—the cube no larger than the tip of his thumb had been popped out of the circuit receptacle. He snatched it up and returned to the Justivac panel. Then he removed one of the viewer units from the base and plugged it into the readout circuit. He placed the cube in position and hastily began to depress the viewer buttons speeding up the concordant readout. He read at a dizzying rate, hardly more than a second or more for each hieroglyph wall. Suddenly he found what he had been seeking. He stopped depressing the buttons and stared, fixing the instructions in his mind.

Then he arose and consulted the schematics. He removed the maintenance tool kit from the service panel and unlocked the panel screws to the main circuit modules. He located the right module and removed it. Then, holding it up to the light, he drew a wire across the switching section and twisted it firmly into place with a pair of needlenose pliers. When this was done, he doublechecked it and replaced the module carefully. Then he checked the meters, saw that the system had not been shorted out, and without further delay, ran out to the Orrery master console where he began to throw all the switches toward the negative poles. At once there was a great throbbing sound, and the floors and walls began to shake.

Doyle watched the readings until the dial needles had been forced down toward the -0 side. He drew a breath of relief and watched as Kagan's image in the viewer went livid with anger. "Why are you doing this?" he raged. "Don't you know it's too late—that the pile is already beyond the slowdown point? Release the circuits or you'll blow this entire planet to bits!"

Doyle smiled at Kagan's panic. He relaxed and depressed the emblem on his communicator ring once again, making contact with Boden.

"I've done it, sir. I've reversed the circuitry and overloaded all systems. Kagan is screaming that it's too late."

"He may be right," Boden said grimly. "We can feel the earth tremors all the way over here. You'd better stay where you are and continue monitoring. What are your orders?"

"For the present, stay where you are. I must see what Kagan is up to. I have a feeling this was too easy, that something else may be . . ."

Before he could finish, the vaulted door at the far side of the domed room opened and a column of armed servoguards stormed in, their weapons leveled at him. Completely caught off guard, Doyle stood transfixed, immobile. He could not believe his eyes. He was certain he had destroyed Kagan's servotroops, but this . . . Where had they come from and who had sent them?

"Doyle? Doyle!" came Boden's voice over the communicator. "What's the matter? What happened?"

Doyle said woodenly, "Servotroops. An entire company of them. Who dispatched them? Who could have known?"

The commander of the servos stopped before Doyle and said in an icily stilted voice, "Do not resist or you will die. Come with us."

Doyle surrendered. He had no other choice. He fell into step behind two guardsmen and glanced around. The others, their weapons pointed at him, followed in ranks of three. They marched rapidly through the vaulted doorway along a circular corridor that seemed to snake around the outer portion of the complex. They finally halted at a transport tube station. Two servos behind him prodded him into the cab. Doyle entered and the door slammed shut. Alone in the narrow confines of the coffinlike tube, he felt himself being hurtled through space. Scant seconds later the tube came to a jolting halt and the door reopened. He found himself facing twenty armed servoguards who were standing in firing squad formation, their cyclonders in the aim position, their fingers on the triggers. He was on the ground level of the hall of the Justivac. Before him glowed the concordance keystone. The squad marched backward in the formation of an inverted arrowhead. One man lowered his weapon and snapped to attention. His wooden face turned to Doyle. His hand lifted and he pointed toward the concordance keystone.

Doyle's footsteps echoed hollowly in the chamber as he walked to the keystone. From above, the cycling spheroid began to descend. He felt the laser light beaming down, encircling him in a cage of shimmering light bars.

He was addressed by a voice that he could not quite recognize though it sounded strangely familiar. "Commandant Doyle you are charged with high treason against the state of Mnemosyne. How do you plead—guilty or not guilty?"

"Not guilty," Doyle said.

"Not guilty plea is unacceptable," uttered the voice.

"I'm sorry about that," Doyle said, "but I'm not guilty.

Instead I charge the state of Mnemosyne with tyranny and treason against its citizens."

The spheroid vibrated and ascended several yards. There was a loud humming sound, and once again the voice was heard, "Such charges are unacceptable. You are guilty as accused, and you are hereby sentenced to be recreated as a servoman. That is all."

Before Doyle could step off the keystone, the guards had formed a circle around him and were closing in, their weapons now holstered, their hands raised as though to grasp him.

He spun around and shouted, "Remember, I'm to be recreated as a servoman. You must not attack me or kill me. I am to be recreated as a servoman." With that, he lunged forward and dove to the floor, tumbling as he moved, his feet kicking aside the two men closest to him, bowling them over. Then he ran for his life toward the transport tube. He squeezed through the door a split second before it closed and hammered on the lighted panel. He removed one of the keys from his pocket that he had used to unlock the door to the memory bank and began to drive it into the light panel with all his strength. Suddenly the lights began to flash and sparks flew in every direction. He jumped back and poised himself at the door, waiting for the transport tube to come to an emergency stop as he guessed it had been programmed to do. As he had hoped, the tube jerked to a sudden halt. The door flipped open and he stepped out, finding himself in a section of inner floor that he judged to be just below the Justivac's memory banks. As an added precaution, Doyle reached inside the transport tube and jerked the key out of the circuitry. At once the sparks stopped flying and the lights ceased flickering. The tube began to hum, and he pulled his arm out just as the door slammed shut and the tube slid away, hurtling downward again.

For the moment free again, Doyle wiped perspiring hands on his clothing and began to walk stealthily toward the far end f the inner floor, which was a space filled with arched girders little more than nine feet tall. He looked up, searching for a way of escape, not daring to think that time was running out and that the odds were stacked against him. Not daring to think that he had underestimated the Secretariat and had not considered the possibility that he had somehow overlooked the main headquarters, he continued relentlessly on. Somewhere he had to locate the connectors that led down from the base of the Justivac to the cycling spheroid, which he was now positive held the key to the mystery.

After groping through the forest of arched girders for more than an hour, Doyle finally came upon a sealed malehole in the side of a building block of cementized plasma. He removed one of the keys from his pocket and used it to pry up the gasket. Then he used his pocket knife to slice away the fibers that had been fused to the closure. When he had cut enough away from the sides and bottom of the circular plate, he put his shoulder to it and forced it inward. He looked down and saw below a gleaming object at the bottom of a narrow shaft. There were no ladders or handholds with which to climb up or down. The circumference of the cylinder was perfectly round and about five feet in diameter. Although the perspiration was freely oozing from his pores, Doyle did not pause to rest or refresh himself. He stepped over the bottom of the opening and eased himself down. Then he swung his legs out and braced his shoulders against the side as he stood horizontally, all his weight depressed against the perpendicular walls of the vertical tube. He began to walk, one step at a time, moving downward toward the shining disc at the bottom. He knew what would happen if he made one misstep. He would fall to his death sixty feet below. He also knew what would happen if by chance something fell from his pockets and warned those below that he was approaching. They could activate the spheroid and send it moving upward in the cylinder and crush him.

149

His muscles ached, and every nerve in his body quivere from the exertion as he descended, step by step. He tremble in the chill sinking air that sucked downward against h sweating body, and he forced himself to think of another tim and another place when he had been in a similar predicamen

He recalled that day in space seventeen years before whe he had climbed out of the airlock above the space transpo and groped his way hand over hand toward the reactor engine that would not shut down and had continued the doubling c the craft's speed through space until they were almost at th point of disintegration due to the time warp versus light spee Just when he had felt he could cling to the body of the vehicl no longer, he reached his goal, the reactor. Then, exerting a almost superhuman effort, he had managed to lock th spanner against the lock nut and freed the shutdown mecl anism. At once the velocity began to decrease, and by the tim he returned to the airlock, the speed had decreased to half th speed of light.

Then, as now, Doyle thought of but one thing—survival. H had to succeed in his efforts or else die in the attempt, and h had no intention of dying. There was too much at stake—to much to live for. Now that he had come this far, and now tha he had been convicted by the Justivac, he knew there woul be no other way to survive except by emerging victor over th enemy.

After what seemed like hours, but was actually only fiftee minutes, Doyle slumped exhausted at the bottom of th cylinder on the spheroid's domed roof. He rested his throbbin shoulders, arms, and legs and used the time to study th construction on which he now found himself. A series o locking nuts to the far side of the spheroid seemed to seal manhole similar to the one he had entered from above. Befor undertaking the effort, he listened intently for some sound some sign of life from below. It would not do if there wa anyone inside the spheroid when he attempted to get it. H surmised the spheroid was remote-controlled and also hoped it contained a crawl space that would lead him to his goal.

He fell to work on the nuts with the pocket spanner, using all his strength to open them. One by one they came loose, and when they were all free, he pried up the cover and removed it after checking below to make certain no one was inside.

Below him he saw a platform similar to the bridge layout of the Orrery. No one was there. He drew a deep breath and then lowered himself through the opening. There was just enough room inside to stand. He looked around and then examined the console panels. The switches were preset to remote operation. He recognized the designations readily. They were similar to the ones on consoles he had used frequently when he had served in the chartmaking complexes out on the frontier. This console was of simple design, and he now felt a surge of confidence that he was getting closer. But to *what*, he did not know, nor could he hazard a guess. It was certainly not Kagan, and it was not the three men he had subdued in their sleep. Who then could be behind it all?

Doyle forced himself to stop thinking. He had one thing to do now—and that was to find the way out. Immediately he began searching for the crawl space and within a few minutes located it beneath the console seat. He pried up the framework of the upholstered seat and saw a ladderlike girder affixed to a small tablet. He crawled into the opening and flattened himself in the rounded portion at the bottom of the spheroid. The tablet was a miniature transport panel. He touched one of the buttons and waited. There was the faint humming sound of an approaching tube hurtling toward him. He drew back and waited. A few moments elapsed and then the tube slammed to a silent stop. The cylindrical door slid open, revealing an upholstered couch inside. He climbed down into it and touched the green button. There was a sensation of motion for several moments, and then the transport tube halted with such

151

force that he would have been knocked unconscious had it not been for the padding that cushioned his head.

The door opened and he looked out. He was in a vaulted chamber that smelled unpleasantly of overheated power units. He guessed he had arrived at the reaction station somewhere beyond the Orrery complex. The power units that he had reversed had most likely caused the strong acrid odor he smelled. Cautiously, he emerged from the tube and walked about, keeping close to the domed walls. At the far side of the cavernous vault was a glassized window through which flickering blue lights could be seen. He crept toward it, and after making doubly certain he was not being observed, he looked through the window.

Below, in a gigantic chamber in which turbines hundreds of feet tall were located, were dozens of men in white uniforms marching along the catwalks. Elevators carried some-of the men up and down. To the right and high above the mountainous machinery was a control tower similar to the Orrery bridge. He saw several figures moving about inside the blue-lighted interior.

Doyle wondered what it all meant. He flattened himself against the wall, and closed his eyes for a moment, unable to comprehend the vastness of the complex beyond, unable to understand how such an enormous project had been erected without his knowledge.

Then it dawned on him.

He knew now how it had all come to pass. The citadel opposite was manned by servomen—citizens of Mnemosyne who had vanished from the face of the planet only to be recreated as slave laborers with their technical skills intact, but their wills enslaved by the masters of the new order. He did not know who was responsible for this. It was inconceivable to him that any human mind or collective body of minds would dare attempt a scheme of such magnitude.

His heart felt heavy when he came to the realization that he was one man alone against a uniquely powerful machine. How had such a thing been accomplished in such a short span of time? And why had it been done? What was to be gained? Why? Why? He asked himself over and over.

Suddenly from out of nowhere a blanket of plasma descended like a gigantic mass, enveloping him in its folds. He felt its oppressive heat and stifling presence as the free-moving glob of translucent matter surrounded him and began to encase him, at first giving him room to move and breathe, then slowly narrowing the space until he could almost reach out and sink his arms and legs into the pulsating mass. He had heard that such a weapon existed on the planet, but until that moment had not believed it. There were some who had said that a member of the Secretariat had developed it and had frequently employed it to keep the other members of the Secretariat in line. When Doyle had heard this, he thought that such an idea was preposterous. How could anyone know what the Secretariat was up to since the membership was such a highly guarded secret?

"Commandant Doyle!" a voice thundered from all around him. "Surrender yourself."

Doyle remained where he was, clinging to a girder high above the abyss. Below him the gigantic machines were humming, and a greenish glow emanated illuminating the billowy form of the plasma. The plasma mass seemed to be closing in.

He said nothing and remained where he was, holding fast to the girder. Something was familiar about the voice that had called him. He knew the voice was being beamed to him through the plasma mass. He decided not to reply, but to wait it out. He fought to keep his nerves calm, knowing it would be fatal if he panicked or lost his head.

"I know you're there, Commandant Doyle. I'm tracking you. I have you surrounded."

The voice was that of Lieutenant Webb! Doyle was stunned

by the realization. He had wondered what had happened to him since their return from the frontier. The lieutenant had been a spy for the Secretariat. He was certain of it now. In all probability he had been given the task of keeping a close watch on him.

"Give it up, Doyle," the encompassing voice said. "You haven't a chance. Surrender, and you will be permitted to live. Fight me, and you will die."

Doyle removed one of the miniature oxygen packs and placed the cup around his face. He waited until the suffocating folds of the plasma closed him into a bubble before turning on the air. Then he doubled over and pretended to be unconscious. He saw the bubble begin to ascend. It rose several levels and then moved along until it reached a security sphere. It drew alongside the airlock and stopped.

After several minutes the airlock door opened and two servoguards emerged. They lifted Doyle's body and carried him inside. They deposited him on the floor of a small chamber in which a control board occupied two of the walls. The servoguards backed away and departed through an exit behind the control board.

Doyle continued to feign unconsciousness. He lay on the floor where they had deposited him without moving. He kept his eyes closed but did manage to peek and get a fix on the situation. He decided he was in a remote guard station. He realized that Lieutenant Webb was undoubtedly in charge, and when this thought occurred to him, his hopes soared. He knew Webb well enough to understand the way he thought. Webb had always been the sort of fellow who delighted in hogging all the glory and taking all the credit. When Doyle had been honored and feted for the defeat of the alien invaders, Webb had been beside himself with envy. He felt he deserved some of the rewards and the plaudits too. Doyle had known this, but had not thought about it. He had been in command and Webb had been his second in command.

Now it hit him. What if Webb had not informed the Secretariat that he had snared him in the plasma blob net? What if Webb was now planning to interrogate him in hopes of learning something of the Chamberist movement. If Webb could learn facts vital to the Secretariat, there would be no doubt that he would receive a commandant's post as a reward.

Doyle dared to glance around the security sphere. There could not be a more desolate, lonely, out-of-the-way place to send a man than this place, Doyle decided. Knowing Webb as he did, he also knew that Webb had most likely fed his hatred on being there by blaming him for it. While Doyle got the glory, Webb got the worst post on the planet. Was this not reason enough for him to want to have Doyle at his mercy?

The appearance of Lieutenant Webb at that moment and the expression on his face confirmed Doyle's convictions. "Now it's *my* turn to get even with you," Webb said, standing over him.

Doyle sat up and pushed himself to his feet. He confronted Webb without blinking. "What do you mean—*get even?*"

Webb laughed. His eyes were narrowed in hatred as he said, "You were responsible for having me transferred to this forsaken sphere, and now you're going to pay for it. If you're wise, Doyle, you'll confess everything you know about the plot to overthrow the regime. If not, you'll suffer the consequences."

"I don't know what you're talking about."

Webb pointed around him. "You're the one who doesn't know what *he's* talking about. I've been cooped up in here ever since we returned from the plains. They gave me this post because you wanted me out of the way while you got all the glory. When you tell me what I want to know, I'm going to use that information to buy my way out of here."

"You're talking through your helmet," Doyle said.

Webb smiled. "Am I? We'll see about that." He turned and pointed a signal pencil at the control panel input. Before he

155

could activate it, Doyle leaped at him. He smashed down his hand and knocked the signal pencil out of Webb's grasp. Then he drove the point of his elbow into Webb's throat. Without a word, Webb dropped.

Doyle knelt beside him and stripped off his cyclonder belt. He tied him securely with it and then gagged him. Then he dragged him toward the console and lashed him securely to the chair.

After Webb was secure, Doyle went to the control panel and proceeded to short out all the circuits. He then pressed the servo command box and told the servoguards, "Open the airlock and march out in single file."

He went to the second airlock door and opened it. The vacuum outside was stifling, and he had to back away and retrieve his oxygen mask in order to breathe. He watched without pleasure as the servoguards stepped out and dropped to their deaths thousands of feet below in the yawning, black abyss.

Then he closed the airlocks and returned to the gasping Lieutenant Webb. He removed Webb's gag and fed him some oxygen. Webb sucked in the life-giving air hungrily. Then Doyle removed the mask and stood glaring down at Webb. "How long have you been spying on me?"

Webb was reluctant to answer. He avoided Doyle's probing gaze by averting his eyes. Webb was a stubborn man, always had been. Doyle knew he could break though. Webb loved life too much.

"Okay, I'll open the airlock, and you'll never have a chance to say anything again."

Webb glared, hatred evident in his expression.

Doyle made a move toward the airlock door release.

"No! What do you want to know?"

"How long have you been spying on me?"

"For as long as I've been back from the frontier. They recruited me to keep an eye on you."

"Whose orders did you follow?"

"Kagan's. He's in charge of national security. He has spies everywhere. They spy on every commander in all the commands of every branch of service."

"Who told you that I was responsible for sending you to this desolate outpost?"

Webb blinked and looked at him. "Are you trying to say you had nothing to do with it?"

"Does it matter now if I didn't?"

"It's too late for that."

"Who told you that lie?"

"Kagan. He told me. He also said I deserved to be sent here because I had failed to get anything on you."

"Get anything on *me?*"

"Yes. The idea was to find one of the skeletons in your closet. That's the way he controls people—gets them to do what he wants them to do. Blackmail is a surefire way of keeping men under his thumb."

"Did you report that you had taken me prisoner?"

Webb smiled. "I ought to have. None of this might've happened if I had."

"You wanted the glory of capturing me all to yourself."

"You might say that."

"I'll make a deal with you, Webb. Are you interested in saving your skin?"

"Yes, of course."

"But I don't know if I can trust you."

"Try me. Just let me live—and let me loose."

"Okay. Give me your word you'll remain here out of touch with the Secretariat and with Kagan until I send someone to rescue you."

"You have my word."

"All right. I'm going to deactivate your communicators and smash them if I must. Then I'm going to leave. I've a job to do, and I want no interference from you or anyone else until that job is done."

"What job?"

157

"Never mind that."

"But I *do* mind. What job?"

"You'll see. When it's over, you'll know all about it."

"Okay. You win. I'm out of the chess game. Untie me and go."

Doyle went to the control board and fired several bursts from Webb's cyclonder at the communicating gear. He went to the lockers and checked them, then moved toward the airlock, taking the flying belts with him. He strapped one of the belts on, fastened the shoulder brace, and gravely saluted Webb as he opened the door and stepped out into the blackness.

When he cleared the open area of black space, the air was too thin to use the belts so he alighted on the top of the inner sphere and discarded them. High above he saw the airlock of the security sphere close. He smiled. Webb had worked himself free and had saved himself. To be sure, Doyle had had no intention of untying Webb. But now that he was imprisoned in the sphere, he had nothing to fear from him.

14

Oscillostat

Doyle emerged from the observatory high above the gigantic turbines and the catwalks below. He had donned one of the white coveralls and anodized lead face masks that he had found in a locker out on one of the catwalks. He tried his best to move about in the same mechanical manner that characterized the servomen and the deliberate jerky movements annoyed him. If he might successfully masquerade as one of the servos and walk about as though following orders, he knew he would eventually find some way to stop the Secretariat. So far he was quite confused by all he had seen; not because he could not understand how all this had been accomplished, but because he could not imagine how the Secretariat had illegally done so much without the people of 143 rising up in protest. He could not believe that the citizens of Mnemosyne had become so docile and complacent that they had allowed all this to happen. He wondered if such people were worth risking his life for. Was it worth it?

Deciding he would have to answer that at another time, Doyle began his methodical exploration of the turbine complex. As he passed crews of servomen at work on the catwalks repairing the circuits he had caused to burn out due to the overloads, he had to force himself to walk with deliberate woodenness, for he knew the scanners were operating, observing every inch of the area.

After descending to the main level, he walked toward the citadel, hoping to find some way of entering unnoticed and then ascending to the control tower high above. Just as he reached the doorports, a servocommander came toward him and depressed a hand controller. "Stop, I say!" the commander said.

Doyle stopped. He froze in his tracks and stared straight ahead.

"What is your sequence?"

Doyle groped for the right answer. He knew what might possibly happen to him if the wrong reply was made and if he hesitated too long. He mumbled, "Zero-six-one-zero."

The servocommander held up a log sheet and scanned it. He did not find such a number on the list. He seemed puzzled and for a moment stared at Doyle's mask. Then he said, "Advance to the programming area. You must be one of the relief force."

Doyle passed inside and continued along a brilliantly lighted passageway. He stopped at the transport tubes and glanced about without turning his head. No one gave him a second glance, if they glanced at him at all. Everywhere were servos coming and going, some carrying coils of cable, others tools and repair kits. Here and there the gold uniform of a servocommander was seen, but they did not notice Doyle, for he was dressed like all the others.

He depressed the transport button, and a tube arrived immediately and he stepped into it. He pressed the uppermost button and seconds later arrived at the top of the citadel. He went out and paused before two servoguards who were posted at the control tower entrance. Through a glassized window beyond the entrance he saw three men seated at consoles, taking readings from a bank of meters and power level dials.

Doyle boldly approached the guards and told them,

"Report to the programming center. You are needed by the servocommander."

For a moment the guards were immobile. Then they lowered their cyclonders and started to obey. Doyle snatched one of their weapons and yanked it toward himself. He turned and depressed the trigger. The servos vanished in a puff of blue light.

Doyle swallowed hard. He now knew there was no way out except through the total destruction of the complex. But how was this to be accomplished? He was no closer to the truth than when he had first set out. It did not make sense to him. Someone was giving orders—but who? And where were the headquarters?

He entered the control tower and moved about mechanically, walking unnoticed. He recognized the scanning devices encircling the area and then pretended to stumble and trip to the deck. As he rolled, he brought the cyclonder up and held the trigger until he had blasted the scanners out of existence. He came up, still firing, destroying the servomen at the consoles and everything in sight. Then he backed away from the complex control area and moved into the corridor, firing again and again at the nodules containing the scanners.

Suddenly great whining sounds began to pierce the air. Doyle began to walk woodenly, like a typical servoman. He reached the end of the corridor and continued on until he arrived at the crossover that led to the adjacent citadel. He stopped and took his bearings. Below, the turbines were afire and the servomen were rushing about attempting to escape. To his right he saw the Justivac citadel, and stretching across the black span high above the abyss, he saw an arched bridgework, which he decided to explore.

Five minutes later he was at the citadel, but this time high above in a chamber that, from its configuration, he knew was just over the Justivac. Doyle wasted no time in finding the way in. Without discarding his coveralls or mask, he climbed down a vertical ladder and went through a passageway. It was the chamber above the spheroid, which he had been unable to enter before because he had not realized it existed.

When he reached the end of the passageway, he peered about for a moment and then entered a dimly lit console center. He realized he had at last reached the nerve center of the Secretariat. Before him was the master console—the unit that was connected to the Orrery! He had no reason to doubt that the search was at an end. All that he needed to do was trace the corridor that led away from the master console to its terminus. There he hoped to find the real mastermind behind the system.

Doyle, wary of scanners and sensor devices, proceeded along the seemingly endless corridor with his cyclonder held at the ready and the trigger set on the destruct phase. When he reached the end, he found himself in a deserted passageway before a single transport tube. He decided not to enter it, reasoning that sooner or later those he sought would return to the deserted master console. He carefully fashioned several sensing devices and placed them on the metallized seams of the corridor. Then he returned to the master console area and found a niche behind the electronic gear in which he curled up and took a well-earned rest.

The faint buzzing of his communicating ring, which he had activated to go off when the sensors he had placed in the corridor were approached, awakened him abruptly. He reset the cyclonder to the paralyzation phase and settled down to wait.

Two men entered the area and approached the console. One was Kagan. The other, he was shocked to see, was Boden, Petra's grandfather!

When he got over his initial surprise, Doyle tried to figure it out. He found the answer with a little thought. Boden had pretended to defect to the underground, but in reality had

162

gone over to them in order to be in a better position to take over when the Secretariat was overthrown. In this fashion he would be able to know the strengths and weaknesses of both factions; hence he would be in the enviable position of defeating both and taking over the reins of government himself.

Doyle fought the inclination to show himself and take Boden and Kagan into custody. He knew they could deny his allegations, and without proof the underground might believe Boden and that would most certainly prove fatal. He would need proof and he would need witnesses. As he mulled this over, he realized that Boden had been working for years to convince the kinsmen in the underground movement that he was on their side and it would be his word against Boden's, which would not be good enough. What Boden had to gain from all this, Doyle had no idea. He thought about Petra and knew that she, least of all, would believe what he had to say.

Doyle, facing his dilemma in calm deliberation, decided he needed to play for time. He would first need to sabotage the entire scanning network. Once that was accomplished, he would be free to move about without being detected. Then he might return to the underground and make a try at getting them to listen to what he had to say.

He had no other choice. He remained concealed behind the console, watching as Kagan and Boden carefully went over the system and quietly discussed how they might reactivate the pile again without too much loss of time and motion. "I see no other alternative," Boden said to Kagan, "except to wait until it cools and then we can inject new energy cylinders. For the present, go back to the Orrery bridge and continue monitoring the console. I'll wait here until you can adjust these maladjusted power level circuits that fool Doyle sabotaged."

Kagan hurried out and jogged down the corridor and out of sight. Doyle settled back to watch. He decided he would follow Boden in order to find out how he had been able to come and go from the underground complex without being seen. A while later he heard Boden speaking over the communicator to Kagan. "You have it now. Very well, I'll secure this console and go back. I don't want them to suspect me at this late stage of the game. Suppose we rendezvous here again at 0100 hours?"

Doyle heard Kagan's voice crackle in the tiny communicator, and then Boden locked the switches. The elder man strode away, and when Doyle heard him making the turn in the corridor, he emerged from hiding and went to the master switch above the scanning viewer control panel. He had learned from the concordance that the scanners and the entire surveillance network would be sabotaged simply by overloading the circuits at the terminus. He grinned with satisfaction as he opened the panel and ripped out the circuit breakers, causing all the power to flood into the lines at once. The overload worked swiftly and efficiently, and all the viewing scopes immediately went blank. The damage he had accomplished with that one simple stroke would take weeks to repair. With a surge of confidence that he was almost there, Doyle strode down the corridor, staying far enough behind Boden to avoid being seen or heard.

Boden arrived at the end of the corridor and then the footsteps ceased. Doyle listened, straining his ears. He did not hear the transport arrive or depart. Instead, there was a faint humming sound, a metallic thud, and then silence.

He ran silently the rest of the way along the corridor. At the end he was momentarily stymied. How could Boden have left the area without departing in the transport tube?

He could not understand it. He removed the mask and pressed his ear to the bulkhead. Somewhere far away he heard the familiar sound of a transport door opening and then closing. The sound was very far away, as though it had come from another world.

Doyle searched every inch of the corridor end. He saw no

way out, no seam, no duct, no secret doorway in the building blocks or in the bulkhead. Then, just as he was about to give up, he leaned against the corridor wall, and there was a whirring sound, followed a moment later by the lifting of a wall panel that had been so ingeniously fitted it had defied detection. Doyle, grinning at his good fortune, stepped through the panel and found himself at the transport tube. He touched the activation button, and moments later a tube arrived to transport him into the depths of the planet.

With his weapon ready to fire, Doyle got into the tube and pressed the single switch. He was rocketed through the environs of the citadel and jerked to a sudden halt deep beneath the ground level, which he was able to determine because the increasing pressure had caused his ears to pop several times. The door opened, and he stepped out into a cavern hewn of solid granite. Ahead was a tunnel. He went toward it and then, bowing his head, passed inside, following it for what seemed like several thousand yards. At last he reached the terminal, a ducted area that turned off in several directions. Doyle did not know which way to turn. He decided to go to his right. As soon as he stepped through the opening three underground guardsmen jumped him and disarmed him. Holding a cyclonder to his back, they wordlessly began to escort him down a sloping passageway.

15

Chaos

"We were able to apprehend you as you infiltrated our headquarters because of the oscillostat," Dr. Tayon told Doyle a few minutes later when he had been brought into the kinsmen's secret chambers. "Now tell us, will you—how did you manage it?"

Doyle was grim as he said, "You won't believe me, I know—but I followed Boden. There's a hidden transport tube beyond the tunnel. It leads directly to the master Orrery control concealed high above the Justivac hall."

"Are you saying that Boden is betraying us?"

"Yes."

"Then why in heaven's name didn't you take him into custody?"

"If I had done so, would you have taken my word against his?"

Dr. Tayon peered at Doyle. After a moment's thought he nodded. "Of course. We wouldn't have taken your word for it."

"And if I can prove my allegation—what then?"

"We must call together the council. This is for them to decide. In the meantime, bear with us, Commander Doyle. If all that you say is so, we have much to thank you for."

Doyle did not show any emotion. He said flatly, "How do you account for the fact that Boden's comings and goings are not detected by your oscillostat?" Then, before the doctor could reply, Doyle said, "Isn't it because Boden himself was the one who invented and installed the device?"

"Why, yes! Now that you mention it, he did invent it."

"If you will let me appear secretly before the kinsmen and testify to what I know, I am positive that before the roons rise this day the new order will be overthrown and we'll be a free people again."

"It's too incredible to be true!"

"But it is. You have no idea of what I've uncovered."

"I think I'm beginning to see. However, I'm still not quite certain I should believe you, Doyle. Some of those on the council have been very close to Boden these past years. They have been so friendly—and if they are in this with him—it would be a tragic error to bring you before them."

"All right, then allow me to suggest something." Doyle was intent. He clasped the doctor's shoulders and said, "If I'm wrong, I will willingly submit to recreation as your personal servovalet. If I'm right, then you will know what to do with Boden and his cohorts."

"Yes, we will know what to do with them."

"Good. Now, please listen to me and heed what I say." Doyle proceeded to tell the doctor of all that he had done and all that had happened. When he was finished with the summary, he said, "Take three of your most trusted colleagues and a body of guardsmen and transport yourselves to the terminal at the end of that transport tube. Before you go, place Boden somewhere safe where he can be watched carefully. Then when you follow him later, he will lead you straight to the master control. I'll wager my entire future and my life, if need be, that you will be convinced once you do what I ask."

Dr. Tayon nodded. "Very well, so be it. Now lead me to the place where this transport tube is allegedly concealed."

"Not until you bring along at least three of your colleagues. Only then will I take you there."

Tayon smiled. "You are indeed a most desperate young man." With that, he turned and departed. Several minutes later he came back accompanied by Drs. Nunn and Chinn. Several guardsmen carrying cyclonders followed. Doyle silently led them back the way he had come. When he reached the hiding place where the transport tube was concealed, he promptly showed it to them. Tayon, Nunn, and Chinn were amazed.

"To think that this was built here without our knowledge is inconceivable!" Tayon gasped.

"When you see what's been going on up there inside the outer citadel walls beneath the dome, you'll find that even more inconceivable."

One by one the party left in the tube that rocketed them to the secret base and then returned just as swiftly. They conducted themselves in awed wonder, in silence, as they followed Doyle to the secret console and then crept into the shadows to await the rendezvous hour of Boden's meeting with Kagan, which Doyle had overheard them arrange.

Doyle had been unable to settle in his own mind certain disturbing facts that nagged at his memory. Somewhere deep within the recesses of his mind he felt that something was still awry; that there was yet some unfinished business to conclude that he had not even begun to think about—but he could not as yet figure out what it was.

Waiting, he found his thoughts drifting to Petra. He smiled and wondered what had happened when she had grown weary of remaining in the sonic bed and had left his quarters. He wondered if she had been questioned, if Kagan himself had interrogated her. He had not wanted to place her in jeopardy, but he had not had any choice in the matter. Once he had got going through the inner citadel, there was no turning back. He had to think about all the people on the planet collectively, not just Petra alone.

He smiled inwardly when he thought of her efforts to make him love her, and he wondered why he had been unable to let himself do so. Others of his time and his recalcitrant age had married and settled down—but they had remained youthful and vigorous while their spouses aged and withered away and their progeny also aged and died and they remained forever young. Doyle had avoided thinking of this, for such thoughts were too unpleasant, and somehow he could not relate himself to Petra even though he was extremely fond of her. There had been something all along that had caused him to turn away from her, and he wondered if it had had anything to do with her admission that she had been Kagan's lover. Could he forget such a thing? Doyle wondered.

He thought of her and wondered how she would take the news that her grandfather was the mastermind behind the terrible reign of terror. He decided he would not be the one to tell her. She had been too close to Boden, she had been closer to the old man than if she had been his only living relative, his daughter instead of his granddaughter.

Doyle closed his mind to such thoughts. He looked at Dr. Tayon and the others who were patiently crouching in the shadows, waiting.

Then the sensor he had activated and secreted earlier that day was activated. "They're coming!" Doyle cried, his voice a hoarse whisper.

The footsteps of a man rapidly approaching were heard. Kagan entered and went at once to the console where he began to open the switches and set the dials. After what seemed an eternity of anguished waiting—during which time Doyle had all sorts of fears passing through his mind that perhaps Boden would not show up, or that he had somehow learned that the kinsmen suspected him, or that he had somehow found out that Doyle had laid a trap for him—Boden entered the vast room and joined Kagan at the console.

Dr. Tayon stood up, motioning for the guardsmen to surround the two at the panel. Then he shouted, "Stand where you are and don't move. In the name of the kinsmen you are under arrest for high treason."

Boden and Kagan whirled around. When they saw they were hopelessly outnumbered, they surrendered meekly. Doyle stood to one side of the console, looking on as Dr. Tayon demanded, "Why—why did you do it, Boden?"

Boden grimaced and turned a surly expression toward Kagan. Kagan put his hand to his mouth and yawned. "Will you stop this ridiculous conversation and kill us? Why prolong our misery now that you've caught us red-handed?"

"You are to stand trial!" shouted Dr. Tayon, his gray mane shaking as he confronted them. "Every citizen of this planet must be told the truth—how you and your cohorts betrayed them and forced them into police state slavery. You will pay for your crimes against our society in a manner befitting the likes of you."

Suddenly there was the sound of laughter all around them. It was a woman's laugh, high-pitched and shrill. "If anyone is to learn the truth, Dr. Tayon, it will be you and the fools of the underground council in league with you!"

The guardsmen and the doctors whirled around. They looked up and saw, descending from hand rungs encircling them around the dome overhead, Petra and fifteen uniformed servoguards. "Put down your weapons and surrender!" Petra cried, menacing them with her cyclonder.

One of the guardsmen lifted his weapon. He was not in time. Petra fired one burst, and he vanished in a burst of bluish flame.

Doyle, his mouth open, stood blinking as he watched her

step down to the deck and come toward him. He could neither speak nor think clearly. Finally he swallowed and managed to mutter, "Petra! So it was you all the time!"

"Yes, darling!" she laughed wildly, walking up to him and smirking in his face. "*I* was behind it all the time. Grandpap and I. Wasn't that a dilly? And it's a pity you won't be alive long enough to witness how I shall reign over the entire planet!"

16

Activation

"You had me completely hoodwinked," Doyle admitted with a touch of sadness as he leaned against the console. "Why did you pretend to be with the underground—why did you go to such lengths to make me believe you and Kagan detested each other?"

"It was necessary, Doyle," she said boastfully, "because I wanted you to get the others out of the way. I knew you could do it for us. Then, when the Secretariat was leaderless, all we had to do was step in and take over where we had left off before we duped you into assuming the commandant's post."

"That way *I* would be the scapegoat and everyone would be fooled into thinking *I* had engineered the whole affair. By then it would be too late and you would have energized the ion field and every human being would have become a slave—and there would have been chaos throughout the planet."

She leered up at him, her eyes wild, as wild as her scheme for taking over.

Doyle suddenly turned and held his hand down against two switches. He shouted, "Now it's my turn, Petra. Tell your servos to lay down their weapons or so help me if I can't stop you any other way, I'll blow up this whole planet!"

"Don't listen to him!" Kagan screamed.

"Yes, *do* listen to him!" Boden cried, rushing forward the halting beside his granddaughter, he gasped, "Don't activat that switch, Doyle. The energy pile is in fusion—if you revers the transformers now, the resulting short circuit will blast u all right out of the universe!"

Doyle, nodding to Dr. Tayon, said, "Take their weapons."

"No!" Petra shrieked maniacally, whirling and glarin madly at Tayon. "Doyle won't push that switch—he wouldn' dare."

In a quiet voice Doyle replied, "All right, Petra, as long a you say I'm about to die anyway, I rather like the idea o taking you along with me."

"He means -it, Petra!" Boden said. "Don't goad hin anymore. We've no alternative but to surrender."

"Said like a true gentleman," Doyle said, again noddin toward Dr. Tayon. The doctor gingerly moved forward an approached the servoguard nearest him. He leaned to one sid and then snatched the weapon out of his hands. Th servoguards were all immobilized, looking to Petra for her nex command. Petra was silent. She gazed at Doyle and then bega to weep. "You fool—you big stupid fool! Don't do thi thing—there's still time—there's still a chance for the both o us—together we could hold this world in the palm of ou hands—together we could . . ."

"Sorry, Petra," Doyle said, "that can never be."

From every direction armed guards appeared, surroundin; Petra and Kagan and Boden and disarming the servoguards Doyle and Dr. Tayon remained beside the console for severa minutes after the others departed. Doyle explained how th mechanism and the circuitry could be disengaged and immobi lized. Then after he had placed the failsafe mechanism ir place, he ripped out the relays and placed the power levels or drain.

In silence the two men walked along the parapet above the vast inner wall area overlooking the huge turbines and dynamos, quietly observing the underground's kinsmen as they herded the servopeople together and marched them toward the amphitheaters in the inner city.

From one end of the Mnemosyne to the other the citizenry thronged to the malls and amphitheaters, gathering together for one purpose—to unite under the good Dr. Tayon who had sent out his edict far and wide that the new order was at an end and the Secretariat finally abolished.

That evening as the six red roons illuminated the domed capitol of Pulsar 143 thousands of voices were lifted in shouts of joy when Dr. Tayon informed them that once again they would abide by the mind code and once again they would be free. Then those who had been accused of high treason and conspiracy were taken before the Justivac before the eyes of all. One by one Dr. Tayon read off the charges and one by one the Justivac arraigned the accused.

"Aide Petra," boomed the voice of the Justivac from its new location high above the amphitheater where all could see and hear, "you are the first to be tried. How do you plead?"

Petra, standing on the concordance keystone, turned and looked around her. She stood mute, the sinking wind fanning the white garments she wore as it blew over the domed city.

"How do you plead, guilty or not guilty, Aide Petra?"

Suddenly, Doyle appeared on the stage of the hippodrome and briskly strode forward. "If the court pleases," Doyle said, "I should like to speak on behalf of the accused."

A murmur rippled through the watching crowds. Then a pall of silence descended as the cycling spheroid deliberated.

17

Justivac

The voice of the Justivac finally echoed forth: "Let it not be said that we who labor here do not seek the truth and the administration of justice. The court recognizes Commandant Doyle. You may speak on behalf of the accused, Aide Petra."

Doyle clasped his hands behind his back and stood to Petra's right. Without glancing in her direction, but facing upward at the cycling spheroid, he said, "When we departed from our native earth to colonize this new land, we left behind in the dust that descended from our spaceship all those concepts and philosophies that we were convinced had since time immemorial led the peoples of the world on the path of death and destruction. We cast off the erroneous teachings of old and vowed never again that we should live by the law of vengeance, the concept of an eye for an eye and a tooth for a tooth or a life for a life. We vowed to establish and live by the mind code in which every man is an entity unto himself, and we vowed that he would live by a code that is not only right for him, but that is right for his neighbor as well. Efforts were made to erase from the human consciousness all those false ideals that contributed so much to man's inhumanity to man. These efforts were not made in vain, for thousands upon thousands have been born here who contributed great things to our society, each person living and working and contributing according to the dictates of his intellect.

"We have erased from the intellect by the process of teaching, not by forbidding; we have taught our children first how to remember and then how to reason for themselves. We have not dictated to them how they are to conduct themselves or how they were supposed to relate to others. They were free to make their own choice in whatever pursuit they wished to follow. We glorified the human mind, and we taught love and respect for it. Most of all we instructed, not by rote methods but by intellectualization, and it was through this method that we were successful.

"I stand here before this high court not to beg mercy for or for vengeance against the accused, but rather to plead that justice and only justice be given."

The cycling spheroid throbbed and pulsated as the voice of the Justivac interrupted. "Are you pleading the accused guilty or not guilty?"

"I plead the accused *not* guilty!" shouted Doyle.

At once a great hue and cry was raised from the audience. People rose up in their seats shouting, shaking clenched fists at Doyle.

Doyle turned and lifted his arms for silence. When the audience was finally still, he turned once again and lifted his gaze to the spheroid. "I do not hold with the old concept of vengeance—that the punishment should fit the crime and all those old ideas," he went on. "Neither do I contend that the guilty ought to go free and unpunished. By the same token I also contend that two wrongs do not make a right."

"Explain what you mean, Commandant Doyle."

"Aide Petra is not guilty for the simple reason that society—*our society*—is guilty!"

"Guilty of *what*, pray tell?"

"Guilty of the most heinous crime of all—the sin of omission."

"Omission?"

"Yes. Our society contented itself to surrender more and more of its freedoms as time went by. The sin of omission was committed each time the citizens of 143 remained away from the polls at election time. By this mass apathy and abstention from every citizen's duty to his country to have a voice and to use that voice as his moral obligation to himself, his family, and his fellow citizens, the people of Mnemosyne are the guilty ones, and I hereby accuse myself as well as every other man and woman who did not exercise his right to vote in our elections. In other words, I am the traitor and all those who did not vote are traitors—not Aide Petra alone. She is innocent of any wrongdoing."

"The logic of such a statement is not clear," rumbled the Justivac.

"I beg to differ with the court—it is quite clear. Had we, the citizens of Mnemosyne, exercised our right to vote, and had we not been apathetic and kept abreast of what our government was doing, Aide Petra, First Officer Kagan, and ex-Commandant Boden would not have contrived to take away the power of the Secretariat, which I may also add, had already disenfranchised the citizens of this nation. Since the people of Mnemosyne had already betrayed themselves by handing over their freedoms and willingly allowing themselves to live in a police state, and permitting the wholesale enslavement of thousands of their brothers and sisters who were recreated into servoservants of the state, and permitting the power of many to fall into the hands of a select few, this court cannot in good conscience find the defendant to be guilty as accused.

"I say that society—the people of Mnemosyne who allowed this to happen are to be indicted for wholesale treason; and I say further that the citizens of this planet cannot by any claimed or alleged right contend that Aide Petra was a traitor—to the contrary, she is a heorine!"

179

The audience was spellbound. Not a muscle twitched, not a cough was heard, not a head nodded or turned. All eyes were fixed in Doyle's direction.

The whirring of the cycling spheroid increased. Then it drew to an abrupt halt. The voice of the Justivac, now activated by the sum total of its logic circuits within its vast memory banks spoke again.

"Let it not be said that we who labor here do not seek the truth and the administration of justice with fairness for all. The court is in agreement with Commandant Doyle's accusation and his plea entered on behalf of the accused. The court hereby indicts Commandant Doyle and all those citizens of Pulsar 143 who did not go to the polls when elections were held, and charges them with the crime of high treason by reason that they criminally and negligently abstained from exercising their obligatory right to vote and in so doing, incriminated themselves.

"Let it be known also that Aide Petra, ex-Commandant Boden, and First Officer Kagan, are herewith found to be innocent as charged due to the lack of evidence against them and are dismissed, free to go."

Petra stood dumbly, blinking at Doyle. She reached toward him as though to touch his arm. Doyle recoiled from her and with his head bowed, moved toward the silent audience.

THE WORLD'S MOST SPECTACULAR NEW
COMET HAS ARRIVED! IS IT A MESSEN-
GER OF DOOM FROM OUTER SPACE? OR
A SCIENTIFIC CLUE TO THE BIRTH OF
OUR UNIVERSE?

THE COMET KOHOUTEK

GREATEST FIERY CHARIOT OF ALL TIME

BY JOSEPH F. GOODAVAGE

_____ P248   THE COMET KOHOUTEK   .95

Popular and bestselling
SCIENCE FICTION
FUTURISTIC · HORROR

PARADISE IS NOT ENOUGH, by Michael Elder. First American reprint of a British science fiction bestseller. The technology of two hundred years from now has turned the earth into utopia, but perfection is, for human beings, perhaps the greatest imperfection of all. The idle population has nothing to do but enjoy itself, and pleasure has become a big bore. The last employed people are the actors, who provide the entertainment for the never-ending canned television shows. When even this is threatened by automation, all hell breaks loose—in paradise!

P00034-0—95¢

THE OTHER SIDE OF THE CLOCK, collected by Philip Van Doren Stern. A collection of superb science fiction short stories. Included are such masters as Robert Heinlein, J. B. Priestly, H. G. Wells. The collection includes twelve tales that take the reader both backward and forward in time, the unifying element that is central to the book. Because the span encompasses all of eternity, time passed and time to come, the authors have a wide spectrum in which to work, and give the book a marvelous pace and variety not often found in such collections.

P00036-7—95¢

THE ALIEN EARTH, by Michael Elder. Cut off from his mother ship by a sudden disaster, Trist-space pilot from a far-off planet —is isolated somewhere in deep space. Only one star is within range, and he manages to crash land on one of its planets. He needs help to make repairs before he can lift off for home, but the natives he encounters know nothing of modern science and cannot aid him. Instead they spend all their time fighting each other and people they call "Romans." Through the use of long-sleep pills, he wakens to an even stranger scene 3000 years later, where . . . ? An alarmingly perceptive, prophetic book.

P00043-X—95¢

TALES FROM THE UNKNOWN, by Kurt Singer. This is not only a collection presenting psychic testimony from among the most notable writers of our time, but a pilgrimage to those hidden shrines and altars where the unbelievable is man's doctrine of faith. Through Kurt Singer, a master of the macabre, the reader visits Haiti, to meet a sorceress as well as a priestess of Voodoo; to Russia, where an incredibly beautiful but bewitched emerald affected the history of that nation for three hundred years; to Tahiti, to witness the ritual firewalk; and, in New York City, where witchcraft and worship of the devil have been revived at the Satan Church. Guaranteed to chill, intrigue and entertain.

P00054-5—95¢

CIVIL WAR II, by Dan Britain. A frightening look at what may well be the future of the United States—when the government is confronted by a *coup* by the long-repressed blacks who are in control of the military apparatus of the nation. Mike Winston, a white government official in charge of the "towns" in which the Negroes are forced to live, uncovers the plot—but too late to forestall the inevitable. In the days that follow he is placed in a position where he can help to save the country, or destroy it! A book both exciting and prophetic—you won't be able to put it down until the last page. **P00055-3—95¢**

FIRST CONTACT, edited by Damon Knight. Here are ten masterpieces of science-fiction and fantasy dealing with man's first encounter with alien creatures from outer space. With all the benefits of our science and history we earthlings still seem to find it impossible to communicate effectively. What is to be expected when our people make contact with creatures or intelligences from other worlds? Perhaps the answers to our problems are to be found in these prophetic and exciting stories from the imaginations of such masters of the game as: Leinster, Sturgeon, Asimov, Henneberg, Kornbluth, Heinlein, and H. G. Wells. **P00062-6—95¢**

BEYOND THE CURTAIN OF DARKNESS, edited by Peter Haining. This is probably the most representative selection of horror and fantasy stories ever to appear in an American paperback. All the giants of the genre are included: oldies like Poe, Hawthorne, Bierce and Lovecraft, and current favorites like Bradbury, Sturgeon, Asimov, Highsmith and Kuttner. And there's Harold Lawlor, Fred Brown, Bill Morrow, Mary Shelley, August Derleth, Joe Le Fanu, and many more. Here are axe murderers, blood-sucking creatures, monster-makers, devils and demons, vampires and vultures, and all the weird and nameless horrors loved by all. **P00138-X—$1.25**

NOWHERE ON EARTH, by Michael Elder. Here is superior science fiction with the threat of reality, for this is the odyssey of one very ordinary man, fighting for his family in a world in which rebellion, either in thought or deed, is not tolerated. His story is both engrossing and frightening—it is a story that is just around the corner from today. Roger Barclay is hunting for his wife and newborn daughter, who have disappeared from a maternity hospital. No one will answer his anguished questions, so he turns to an underground group, led by a mysterious revolutionary, for help. What he finds will surprise you. **P00157-6—95¢**

SCIENTIFIC ASTROLOGY, by Sir John Manolesco. Finally, the inside truth about astrology! Here is a clear, authoritative and absorbing look at a very old subject, one that has long been fascinating to both fans and cynics. It is a most unique exploration of an influential force at work on all of our lives. Sir John's book gives outsiders an inside look; the whole truth about astrology: the information necessary to evaluate any given astrological source. **P00176-2—95¢**

DREAM-SCOPE, by Sydney Omarr. Here, from the man named "Outstanding Contributor to the Advancement of Astrology," is a revolutionary method of tapping the world of dreams, of viewing them both in the form of written words and pictures. DREAM-SCOPE allows each reader to embark upon adventures previously confined to the world of sleep. All the mysteries of dream interpretation are revealed, permitting the reader to "see" his dream as he never could before—but always wanted to. From cover to cover, DREAM-SCOPE is a dream of a book.
P00185-1—95¢

FLIGHT TO TERROR, by Michael Elder. Seven people marooned on an enchanted planet! In this exciting sequel to *Nowhere on Earth*, a space crew from earth orbits Roker II—a beautiful, spell-binding planet. A group of experts leaves the ship to search for a small colony of people who have taken up residence there. As they fall towards the planet, the ship that they have left disappears and they quickly become the ones who are in need of rescue. Stranded on this strange planet, these seven survivors suddenly discover the frightening truth about what happened to the first colony. **P00219-X—95¢**

MIND OUT, by Diana Carter. A provocative novel about a far-out communal group. The "Cerebralists" are a group who entice young, alienated, often rather confused young people to join their strange cult. They are then forced to sign over all their property. But to whom? No one knows the leader. He communicates with his members through strange codes and supervises them by closed-circuit TV. There are strange, mind-bending initiation rites, which some do not survive and which leave others in a permanent childlike state. Giselle Baker is the child of a famous, but aging, French movie actress. She is induced to join the group by the first man she meets. What happens to her will frighten and fascinate you. A book no one will be able to put down. **P00220-3—95¢**

THIS IS YOUR ORDER FORM.
CLIP AND MAIL.

_____P00034-0 PARADISE IS NOT ENOUGH,
        Michael Elder

_____P00036-7 THE OTHER SIDE OF THE CLOCK,
        Philip Van Doren Stern

_____P00043-X THE ALIEN EARTH, Michael Elder

_____P00054-5 TALES FROM THE UNKNOWN,
        Kurt Singer

_____P00055-3 CIVIL WAR II, Dan Britain

_____P00062-6 FIRST CONTACT, Damon Knight

_____P00138-X BEYOND THE CURTAIN OF DARKNESS,
        Peter Haining

_____P00157-6 NOWHERE ON EARTH, Michael Elder

_____P00176-2 SCIENTIFIC ASTROLOGY,
        John Manolesco

_____P00185-1 DREAM-SCOPE, Sydney Omarr

_____P00219-X FLIGHT TO TERROR, Michael Elder

_____P00220-3 MIND OUT, Diana Carter

TO ORDER
Please check the space next to the book/s you want, send this order f
together with your check or money order, include the price of the bo
and 25¢ for handling and mailing. to:

PINNACLE BOOKS, INC.
P.O. Box 4347 / Grand Central Station
New York, N.Y. 10017

☐ CHECK HERE IF YOU WANT A FREE CATALOG.

I have enclosed $_____check_____or money order_____
payment in full. No C.O.D.'s.

Name_____

Address_____

City_____State_____Zip_____
(Please allow time for delivery.)